ISBN-13: 978-1-952412-19-6

Cover design: 100covers.com
Published By: Vagabond Publishing
Printed in the United States of America

MEMORY AND SORROW

MEMORY AND SORROW

NOW

The sweat was pouring down my face as I grunted and strained. My hands felt numb, and my arms were shaking as I poured everything into this fight. Muscles were screaming in protest at the abuse, but I couldn't give in. There was too much riding on this. I would not be defeated. Not here. Not today.

With a roar of triumph, I tossed down my weapon and fell backwards to enjoy my hard-earned rest. "You beat it into submission, Dahlish," I said hoarsely, staring up at the popcorn ceiling of my living room. That only started my thoughts swirling around the next project waiting to be done on finally restoring the old house I'd bought nine years earlier during the housing market crash. I'd had dreams of turning it into an updated and comfortable home, and then promptly set the project aside to focus on my job.

Groaning, I rolled over and pushed myself into a sitting position. The sandpaper block I was using to strip the old wood floors before staining and varnishing was on the other side of the room. I stared at it for half a minute, trying to decide if I had enough energy left to walk over, pick it up, and toss it back into the old toolbox I was borrowing.

"Tomorrow," I promised. The light coming through my uncovered windows was already growing dimmer as the sun continued a steady descent. I managed to lean over just enough to see the time on the microwave in the kitchen, and cursed. I was going to be late if I didn't get a move on.

I stayed in the shower longer than I'd planned, enjoying the way the hot water worked to loosen up muscles already tightening from unfamiliar strain. After twenty minutes, I reluctantly turned off the water and toweled off as quickly as I could. My thermostat was set at 68° for the winter, and I could feel myself shivering after the warmth of the hot shower.

A quick look in the mirror confirmed that I really needed to shave, but I didn't have time for that. The bristly week's growth of black scruff helped to highlight my light blue eyes. I knew the person I was heading out to meet wouldn't be bothered by it. She'd probably enjoy it, in fact. I couldn't help but grin at the thought of it.

After pulling on a pair of jeans and plain black t-shirt, I grabbed some socks and retreated to my bedroom to search for the comfortable running shoes I liked to wear when I wasn't going out on a job. One was under the bed, and it took a while to find the other buried under an old hoodie that I'd tossed into the room earlier in the day after a trip to the home improvement store.

I combed back my dark hair with my fingers as I stuffed my wallet and keys into pockets, then took a last look around the bedroom to make sure I wasn't forgetting something. Other than cleaning the room, which I'd been forgetting to do for nine years now. That chore could wait a while longer. After all, I'd be forced to clean it when I finished the floors in the rest of the house and started on the bedroom.

The last red streaks of sunset were fading from the sky as I slid into my comfortable old Honda and pressed the button to start the engine. As long as traffic cooperated, I'd still be on time. I didn't have to go far, and stuck to residential streets for most of the trip. It was Friday, so a lot of people were heading out to enjoy a night out after the work week. But it was also January, so the cold would keep some inside their warm homes.

It was still a few minutes before six when I parked at the curb, in front of a tidy house near the middle of a street full of older homes. The neighborhood had a charm that was missing in most of the cookie cutter new construction being slapped up all around the outer edges of the city and in the growing sub-urbs. I won't lie and say I hadn't been tempted to buy one of the newer homes, though. I was quickly realizing that I hadn't inherited the handyman genes from my parents, who used to love working on crafts and projects around the house I grew up in.

I ran my hands through my wild hair a few more times as I walked up the cracked concrete path to the screened front door. Pausing there, I took a deep breath and then pulled the screen door open. I rapped my knuckles on the wooden door, three times in quick succession. My hand hadn't even had time to fall back to my side before the door swung open almost vio-lently.

"Jack!" a voice shrieked excitedly as arms wrapped around my knee in a tight hug.

"She's been waiting by the window for the last half hour," Anna said, standing a few steps away. Her eyes were on her daughter, smiling happily to see the girl's simple joy.

"It's always good to have someone looking forward to seeing me," I told her with a grin, as I bent down to get a real hug. It had been a little over a month since I was hired to find the kidnapped child. When I found her and seven other girls being held in the home of a lamia, a variety of the supernatural Filii Nox, little Penny had latched onto me and still showed no signs of letting go.

Amalia, the girl's grandmother and the woman who had pleaded with me to find her, had invited me to a barbecue to celebrate Penny's return the day after the rescue. I'd gone expecting to never see them again, like most of my other clients, and been surprised when Anna called me up a few days later asking if I'd like to visit. Penny had been begging her mother to let me play in the park with her, the same park she'd been abducted from in early December. From there, I'd fallen into a habit of visiting once or twice a week to share a meal with the family, or to take Penny to the park and give her mother some time alone.

I pulled back from the girl's embrace and looked into her happy eyes. "How's my favorite three-year-old doing?"

"I'm not three!" she yelled, laughing. "I'm four!"

"What?" I made my eyes wide in shock. "When did that happen?"

"Today," Penny said proudly. She held up four little fingers, struggling to keep her thumb down. "I'm this many now, Jack."

"That's amazing," I told her, pulling a hand from behind my back with a small, wrapped parcel. "In that case, I should give you a gift. Happy birthday, Penny!"

The girl shrieked with delight, ripping the paper from the box even as her mother told her to be careful. Soon she was pulling a silver chain from the velvet interior of the jewelry box. Penny held the necklace up to her mom, showing off the small talisman hanging from it that was a half-sized copy of the one I wore around my neck at all times. "Mommy, Jack got me a necklace!"

"It's beautiful," Anna said, looking at me with gratitude. "Do you want me to help you put it on?"

Penny handed over the necklace and turned without a word, jumping from foot to foot impatiently as her mother secured the clasp of the chain behind her neck. The little girl held the talisman up, staring at it with her tongue poking between her teeth in concentration. "It looks just like yours," she said, turning her attention back to me.

"I know how much you like mine," I said, pulling it out from my shirt so Penny could compare it with hers. "Now we're twins!"

She giggled at that, reaching out to rub a hand along my bristly cheek. "We're not twins, Jack. I'm a little girl, and you're old."

"Yep, that's me. I'm the ancient old man that's going to keep an eye on you tonight." I raised a hand and flexed my fingers. "I'm not too old to tickle you, though." Penny squealed and ran from the room, her laughter fading as she retreated deeper into the house.

I stood from my crouch, cursing the popping knees that told me I really *was* getting old. Anna was chuckling and shaking her head. "You didn't have to get her something so extravagant, Mr. Dahlish." She bent down to pick up the box the necklace had come from, running a finger along the elaborate script of the jewelry store I'd found to make the custom piece.

"Anna, you've got to start calling me Jack. I think we know each other well enough by now." I smiled at her, knowing she'd inherited the formality from her mother. Amalia also refused to call me by my first name. "Where is Emilio taking you tonight?"

"We're going to catch this new rock band playing at a bar on the Riverwalk." I turned my attention to the tall man entering the living room as I stepped fully into the house, closing the door behind me. Emilio was several inches taller than my six feet, and he carried fifty more pounds on his frame. The shaved head and long, braided goatee added to the imposing look. We bumped fists as he passed to grab his coat from hooks beside the door. He then grabbed a pink one, holding it out as Anna slid her arms into the sleeves.

"The munchkin and I will probably watch *Frozen* for the thousandth time," I said. "I know you're jealous, but it's my turn to get to enjoy that while you have to suffer through a fun night out on the town."

"Yeah, I'll try not to cry about missing out on watching Anna and Elsa for the hundredth night in a row." Emilio was smirking, knowing how much I hated that movie by now. The first five times had been good, but then I started waking up from dreams about it and realized I didn't want to have to watch it again. There was no way any of us could tell Penny no, however.

"We'll be back by eleven," Anna said, looking through her purse to make sure she had everything she might need. "I have my cell, so call me if something happens. The chicken nuggets are already in the oven, and the mac and cheese just needs to be warmed up."

"Anna, it's not my first time babysitting. You two get out of here and let me spend some time with my favorite girl." I could see Penny peeking around the corner of the wall, watching us from the hallway that led to the bedrooms. "If she doesn't behave, I'll hold her upside down and tickle her."

Penny shrieked, running toward me with her hands out. "I tickle you, Jack." Her fingers poked at me, trying to tickle my thighs. I laughed, bending down to grab her and tickle her stomach in return.

Pulling her up to sit on my hip, we waved as Anna and Emilio left the house. Once the door was closed, we looked at each other with serious faces. "Okay," I said. "What are we going to watch tonight?"

"Olaf!" she yelled, raising her arms. The animated snowman was her favorite part of the movie, and she'd often make me rewind and play his parts again. She wriggled in my arms until I let her slide down to the ground, and then she raced across the room to turn on the TV and start the movie. With a heavy sigh, I heard the theme music start playing and retreated to the kitchen to start on dinner.

I was still amazed at how much I enjoyed spending time with Penny. I'd never been much for kids, one of those single people who feigned interest when introduced to a friend's new baby or when celebrating first and second birthdays. The therapist the city hired to work with Penny and the other seven girls had told me the connection was a byproduct of our shared traumatic experience. He didn't know the reality of what I'd faced in that house, thinking it was just a crazy woman who was abducting kids, but I couldn't help but think that he'd pegged it correctly.

Part of it, I had to admit to myself, was the fact that Penny reminded me so much of my sister when she was a kid. I'd been five years old when she was born, old enough to still have memories of carefully holding the squirming infant in my arms as my mom introduced me to my new little sister. Jennifer had shown the same enthusiasm and excitement that Penny often did. I spent the summer between second and third grades watching the animated Robin Hood movie over and over, the same way I was now watching *Frozen* for the eighth time in less than two months.

Thinking about my sister sent me down a spiraling path into old memories. Many good, but more of them were sad than I'd prefer. Especially the last memories, reminders of my greatest failure as a brother.

THEN

I sat on my sister's bed, staring down at the purple paper she'd left a note on, not really seeing it. The room around me was immaculate, a stark contrast to the messiness of the rest of the one-bedroom apartment we'd shared for the last few years. I didn't know if I'd been sitting there for seconds or hours, only that I still felt the punch in the gut from reading her sloping handwriting that told me how I'd failed as a brother.

Jennifer was nineteen, almost done with her first year at San Antonio Community College. She'd been dreaming of becoming a CPA for years, loving the math and ability to set finances in order for people who were having difficulties. It was a dream I'd fully supported, knowing she could get a great job with that kind of skillset.

In pursuit of my own ideas of becoming a financial titan and living the high life, though, I'd been ignoring Jen far more than I ever should have. For years I'd worked any job I could get, often two or three at a time while raising my sister and then getting some college courses in. Our parents were killed in an accident six years before. As an eighteen-year-old, the courts recognized me as an adult and allowed me to take guardianship of my thirteen-year-old sister. It had been a hard life, but I'd thought I was handling it pretty well until that moment.

Jen had been trying to tell me something the previous evening, something important. As usual, I'd been too wrapped up in my own plans to even take a minute and listen, promising we'd talk in the morning. When morning came, she wouldn't respond when I called through the door, so I left to start work without a second thought.

Arriving home after work, I found my dirty breakfast dish still in the sink and my clothes from the night before still spread across the floor. My neat freak sister would have tidied up after me automatically, so I was instantly worried. Forcing open the locked bedroom door when there was no response, I found her clothes and a few possessions gone. The note was waiting for me on her bed.

Jack, I'm leaving. I tried to tell you, to explain why. But you didn't have time for me, like always. I appreciate what you've done for me since mom and dad died, but now I have to make my own life. There are some people I know who offered me a job. The money is good. Don't try to find me. I'll call when I'm ready to talk. Jen.

What kind of people had my sister fallen in with? My first thought was drugs, but I have to admit that was purely inspired by her recent love of death metal and the new purple hair she'd been sporting for a few months. I knew Jen was too responsible to do much more than get a hit off a joint being passed around. I wracked my brain for a long time while sitting on her bed. Long enough that it was fully dark when I finally thought to step outside and check with one of our neighbors.

Mrs. Wisson had lived across the breezeway since Jen and I moved into the apartment. She was a prototypical little old lady; gray hair, horn-rimmed glasses with a chain dangling

11

behind her head, bent over in her old age. Thinking back at that moment, I realized I'd never seen anyone visit her in all the time we'd lived next door. Perhaps that loneliness explained her need to keep a constant watch from her windows.

I knocked lightly on her door, afraid I might be waking her. I wasn't sure what time old people went to bed. From the wise heights of my twenty-four years, I felt sure they slept most of the day away since I never saw them out at clubs or restaurants that I went to with my friends. So, I was a little surprised and very happy when the door swung open within half a minute. Mrs. Wisson stared up at me, the blare of a TV game show in the background.

"What do you want, young man?"

"Hi, Mrs. Wisson. I'm Jack Dahlish, from next door?" I turned to point at my door, wondering briefly if maybe the woman had dementia and wouldn't even remember anything she'd seen through her windows.

The old woman stared at me with tightly pursed lips for a few seconds. "And here I thought you were Ed McMahon with my Publisher's Clearing House check. I know who you are, kid. What do you want?"

Wow, sarcasm. I'd thought for sure people lost that ability when the gray hairs started to come in. "I'm sorry to bother you, but I was hoping you might have seen my sister leave today? Or maybe some people coming into our place?"

She shook her head decisively. "Not a peep from your place since you left this morning. Thanks for slamming that door every day and waking me up from one of the few decent bits of sleep I get these days."

"Oh, uh, I didn't realize I was doing that." Now I felt oafish and foolish, and I couldn't help reaching up a hand to rub at the back of my neck. So much for dementia.

"You like to stand on your balcony and yell into that fancy phone of yours, too. I know more about your sex life than anyone should." Her eyes were boring into mine now, and I could feel the red flush of embarrassment spreading across my face. "As for your sister, she's a nice girl. Jen always says hi to me, and she brings me a few cookies whenever she bakes them."

Mrs. Wisson was smiling wistfully now, staring over my shoulder as she indulged in the memories. I couldn't believe my sister had gotten to know the neighbor so well. Not because it was out of character for her; Jen was the kind of person who would sit down next to a total stranger and start talking as if they were lifelong friends who just hadn't seen each other in a while. But she hadn't told me anything about getting to know the old lady next door. Had I really been that out of touch with her?

"It's odd, though," Mrs. Wisson said, raising a finger to tap against her chin. "I did see her leave last night. It was about an hour after you left, slamming that door again."

That grabbed my attention back to the matter at hand. "Last night? Was she with anyone? Did she say anything about where she might be going?" We'd only been able to afford one car, so I had to drive my sister anywhere she wanted to go for years. When she turned sixteen, some of her friends started

13

stopping in to pick her up, but those were rare occasions. For college, she'd been taking the bus to and from the campus since I was at work well before she needed to leave for class.

"I thought she was stepping out with her young man. But he was in a dark jacket with a hood pulled up over his head, so I'm not sure if it was him."

What young man? I wondered. "What young man?" Okay, so I wasn't the smartest tool in the shed. My sister was gone, I'd just been called on my total self-absorbed asshole behavior, and this old lady was blowing away all my preconceptions. Jen had boyfriends, sure, but it had been more than a month since she broke up with the last loser. Had she told me about someone else and I didn't pay attention? Or had she thought I didn't care enough to inform me of what was happening in her life these days?

Mrs. Wisson gave me a look that conveyed she was sharing the same thoughts about my lack of attention to my only remaining family member. "She's been going out most nights after you leave for whatever it is you do. A nice young man usually comes by, knocks on the door, and they drive off in his car. A sensible little car, one of those Prions or whatever they're called. Red, I think."

I was staggered. Even with my nine-hour workdays, I went out most nights to get a drink with friends or just hang out at a club. I always thought of it as stress relief, but I was starting to wonder if it was my selfish way of building a life outside of the crappy apartment I shared with my sister. All the while, Jen had been going out with a boy I'd never met and knew nothing

14

about. Was he the one who talked her into leaving? What kind of situation was she in because of him?

"Did you hear them say anything, Mrs. Wisson? Anything that would help me find her?"

The old woman stared at me again, this time with pity on her face. "She finally left, didn't she?" With a head shake and a string of tsk's, she reached out to place a gnarled hand on my arm. "Jack Dahlish, you left your sister long ago. When was the last time you spent more than a few minutes awake here? Always flitting around here and there, and never taking the time to sit and enjoy the family that you have. Jennifer is a wonderful young woman, but I know how lonely she felt because she would spend so much time talking with me. I'm surprised she stayed as long as she did. I'm sure she'll reach out to you when she's ready."

My mouth was hanging open as I listened. Leave it to the elderly to drop the truth out of nowhere. With a final pat on my arm, the door closed on my face. A few seconds later I heard the volume of the game show turned up as Mrs. Wisson settled into her life again.

Was she right? Would Jen reach out to me when she was ready? I still felt the drive to try and find her, to rescue her from whatever situation she had found herself in. And that brought me another thought that shook my world. *What if Jen found something that's better than our life together, not worse?*

15

<u>NOW</u>

With a snort and shake, I woke to the stillness of my dark bedroom. I'd been having a dream, but the memory of it was already fading. Probably another *Frozen*-inspired concoction. Penny had made me watch the movie twice before she agreed to crawl under her pink princess sheets and listen to me read a story about a mouse and a cookie. By the time Anna and Emilio made it home, the little girl was deeply asleep, and I was feeling pretty exhausted myself.

I finally cracked open one eye, infused with the usual nighttime feeling that I wasn't alone in the room. I'd often wondered what kind of primitive remnant had survived in our brains to make us wake in the middle of the night, sure that something else was lurking nearby. Just waiting for us to make a move so it could attack. For some reason I always felt that if I kept pretending I was asleep, it would go away and leave me alone.

Once the fog of sleep started to lift a bit more, I realized that this feeling was something more. Now I felt even more certain that someone or something was in the house. Breathing as softly as possible, I strained to listen for the slightest sound outside of the normal creaking and popping that randomly filled an old house. My eye roved around the part of the room that I could see through the barest slit, but I found nothing out of the ordinary.

Finally, I rolled onto my back and opened both eyes wide. There was a shadow in the corner of the bedroom, tall and bulky. The nightlight in the bathroom cast just enough light so that I could make out a faint profile of a craggy face. "Nyk," I said, as casually as possible when waking up in the wee hours to find someone in the house who shouldn't be there.

"Jack," came the rumbling reply. I saw the profile dip as he nodded once in my direction.

"What the hell are you doing in my bedroom, Nyk?" I turned my head to look at where my phone sat on a stand while it charged. "At three seventeen in the morning, no less."

"I got offered a job tonight that I think you might want to join me on." Nyk grunted and chuckled. "Well, I guess it was last night now."

Groaning, I rubbed my hands over my face and reached out to flip on the small lamp I kept by the bed. The lightbulb was low wattage, but still bright enough to blind me for several seconds as my eyes adjusted. Once I could see, I pushed myself up into a sitting position to face the bounty hunter. Nyk and I had known each other for many years, and often worked together on difficult jobs. During my last big case, finding the kidnapped girls, he had helped me rule out one of my suspects. In return, I'd tagged along a few weekends later when Nyk was tracking a dangerous man with a big bounty on his head.

Nyk Walsh was one of the few humans in San Antonio who knew about the Nox hidden throughout the city. He'd come to that knowledge a few years before I did, when he was hired to track a minotaur without realizing it. The only reason he'd

17

survived the encounter was because of an old ogre ancestor in his own bloodline. That great-grandfather's height and strength had skipped a few generations before barreling to the fore when Nyk was born as an eighteen-pound infant.

He stood now from his half crouch, his spiky blond hair scraping my seven-foot ceiling. His body was so wide that he had to turn sideways to get through most doors, and his muscles needed separate area codes. Every time I saw him, I instantly thought this was not a man I ever wanted to find on my trail.

"Must be an important job," I said grumpily, "if it merits breaking into my house in the middle of the night and playing creeper in the corner of my bedroom."

The big guy shrugged, and for a moment I worried his shoulders might crack the drywall. This is a man I've seen lift a small car with one hand just because he worried that a cat might have gotten trapped under it. "I'll make coffee and tell you all about it."

I watched him slide through the doorway as I tossed the covers aside with a heavy sigh. No more sleep for me. I'd just have to hope the couple of hours I managed were enough to get me through the rest of the day. I was one of those people who could never take naps, no matter how exhausted or run down I felt. I could count the times I'd fallen asleep in the middle of the day on one hand.

After splashing some water on my face and throwing on a t-shirt over my boxers, I walked into the kitchen to find a cup of coffee already waiting on the counter. Nyk was standing in the wide entry that separated the kitchen and living room, shaking his head as he looked at the mess left behind from my work on the floors.

"You could have borrowed my floor sander, Jack. That would have been much faster." He poked at a pile of dust and shavings with a size twenty boot. "A lot neater, too."

"But then I wouldn't have the satisfaction of doing the job myself," I said, trying to sound as if I believed that. In truth, I'd decided to do the work on the spur of the moment when Anna visited with Penny a few weeks before. The little girl kept asking where I lived, and then looked wholly unimpressed when she saw the state of my house. I didn't even think to ask my few friends if they had tools to make the job easier.

Nyk just shook his head some more and turned away. The entryway was wide enough for two normal people to pass comfortably, but the big man almost filled the space on his own. The coffee cup he was holding looked like a teacup from Penny's little playset in his huge hands, and I wondered if he got more than one swallow from it.

"I've been hired to find the Magpie," he said.

I paused, my own coffee cup resting on my lip as I was about to take a sip of the steaming liquid. My entire body went still, and I felt as if a live wire was buzzing electricity through me. "the Magpie is dead."

Nyk shrugged, again threatening the stability of my house. "That's what I thought, too, but my employer is quite convinced they're not."

"*He's* dead," I said emphatically, setting my cup on the counter angrily. "He's been dead for ten years, and good riddance." A ball of anger and frustration was growing in the pit of my stomach, and I turned away from the bounty hunter to look at the dark window that would show my overgrown back yard in the daytime. The face reflected back looked pinched, with a tight mouth in the middle of a week's worth of stubble. The bags under my eyes and mussed hair made me look more like a homeless person than an investigator.

A giant hand landed gently on my shoulder, and I jumped. Nyk had snuck up on me while I was lost in my own reflection. "I know this is difficult, Jack. It's why I wanted to come to you right away. If the Magpie is still out there, then I know you'll want to track them down more than anyone else."

"I told you, he's dead!" I brushed the hand from my shoulder and stepped away to cross my arms and stare at a blank wall. I felt like a sulky child, but this was one thing I refused to budge on. Because if I was wrong, and the Magpie was still alive, then I'd been living a lie the last decade of my life.

I heard the clink of a coffee cup settling in the sink, and heavy footsteps crossing the small kitchen. "I'll give you some time," Nyk said softly. "Call me when you're ready, Jack. If you don't want to work this one with me, I'll understand."

Once the front door closed behind him, I grabbed my face with my hands and yelled as loudly as I could. It felt good to let all the emotion out, even as I felt my throat being torn by the scream. As soon as the air emptied from my lungs, I took a deep breath and let loose one more time. I also slammed a fist on the scratched formica counter, relishing the pain that radiated through my hand and wrist.

"This can't be happening," I whispered to the empty room. "Jen, I swear I got him for you."

THEN

After talking with the old lady next door, I went through my sister's few remaining emails again, then scrolled through her Facebook page and other accounts trying to find anything that would point me toward a new boyfriend. By the end, I was just happy to have a couple of names of people who commented on her posts more often than others. Maybe they'd be friends that Jen had spoken with offline and could help point me in the right direction.

It was just past two in the morning when I sent off a few emails and private messages to those people, asking them to call me on my cell phone. I told them that Jen was gone, and I was trying to find her, leaving out any other information in hopes that it would fuel curiosity and make them reach out.

After laying on the couch for an hour, trying to fall asleep, I gave up and sat with my head in my hands. I went through my memories of our short conversation two nights earlier, kicking myself yet again for not taking a few minutes to listen when Jen said she had something important to talk about. Instead, I was so wrapped up in my own thing, not wanting to be late to meet some friends for drinks.

Disgusted with myself, I grabbed my keys and left the apartment. I didn't think about my door until after I'd slammed and locked it, wincing at the thought of disturbing Mrs. Wisson so soon after she'd pointed out my bad behavior. In recompense, I tried to walk as softly as possible on the short trip to the parking lot where my dented old mid-nineties Buick was parked. The car had belonged to my parents, one of the few possessions remaining after our old house was sold off to pay the debts left behind.

I drove around the part of town we lived in for hours, cruising up and down streets as I looked at every woman I saw walking or sitting by the side of the road. I kept hoping to see a flash of purple hair, or a familiar graceful gait that would reveal my sister. At the same time, I was desperately hoping not to see her. To instead cling to the hope that she had found a safe place to stay while she worked whatever job her friends had offered.

Several times I picked up my phone and started dialing 911 to report her missing. But each time I stopped before initiating the call, setting the phone aside. My sister was nineteen and legally an adult. If she wanted to leave her shitty brother who couldn't even take five minutes to listen to her when she asked to talk, why would the cops waste time trying to find her? Especially after they saw the note where she told me not to look for her.

When dawn was streaking the sky to the east with shades of orange and red, I returned home and shuffled into my apartment. This time I remembered to close the door gently behind me. I called my boss and left a voice mail that I couldn't make it into work. I'm sure my anemic coughs and sniffles were wholly unconvincing, but I couldn't find the energy to care if he believed me or not.

I was finally drifting down into sleep when a chirping noise startled me back to wakefulness. My hand automatically reached out for the phone, flipping it open to look at the black and white display of the phone number. I was about to decline the call as I always did with unknown numbers, but then I remembered my messages to Jen's online friends. I pressed the green button to accept the call and held the phone to my ear. "Hello?"

"Hi," a young sounding female voice replied. "Is this Jen's brother?"

"Yeah, I'm Jack. You got my email? Who is this?"

"I'm Emily? Emily Firestone? You said Jen is missing?"

I remembered the name Emily, a girl a few years younger than my sister who always posted smilies at the end of every sentence when she replied to one of Jen's posts. "She wasn't here when I got home last night, Emily. Our neighbor said she left with a guy, and I was hoping you might know who that would be. Jen hasn't been sharing the details of her dating life with me recently."

There was a long silence on the phone. I started to wonder if the call had dropped when I heard a faint response. "Do you mean Billy?"

A name! But one I'd never heard before. I tried to remember if I'd seen any emails or posts from a guy named Billy or Bill or William, but I couldn't. "Who is Billy? Did they go to school together?"

"No," Emily said, still faint and sounding very hesitant to even talk with me. I could imagine the conflicting emotions

24

inside of her, wanting to help her friend but also wanting to keep any secrets that Jennifer didn't want revealed.

"Emily, I promise I'm not just being overprotective big brother here." Even though I kind of was, when I thought about it. "I want to find my sister before something happens to her. Please help me do that."

A sigh filled the line. "Billy is a guy she met at a place called Shine a month ago."

"Shine?" I knew it, a supposedly hot dance club just out-side of downtown. One of those run-down warehouse type places that gives the young people a thrill of venturing into the dangerous part of town while also providing security and excellent service. It was also a place that Jen never should have been able to get into for at least a couple more years. "Was this a frequent hang out?"

"No," Emily said, strongly. "Megan's sister got us in once, because she knew the bouncer. She, like, flashed her boobs at him, and he didn't even ask to see our IDs."

"Megan? Is that someone Jen knew from school?"

There was silence again. "Megan is Jen's best friend. You don't know that?"

"I'm a crappy brother, Emily. Obviously. What else can you tell me about this Billy person?"

I could almost hear the shrug through the phone line. "He's just some older guy who latched onto Jen the moment we walked through the door and wouldn't leave her alone. After a while, she seemed to like talking with him." There was a long pause again, and I was about to speak when she rushed through the next sentence. "I saw him pass little paper packets to a few people while we were there."

Great. My sister was hanging out with a drug dealer, and apparently enjoying his company. "Do you know if she saw Billy again?"

"Uh huh. They went out the next weekend, for sure, and I think Jen kept seeing him. She stopped talking about other guys around then, and Megan was convinced she was dating Billy."

Double great. My sister was *dating* the drug dealer. Now I was almost certain this so-called job of hers was going to involve running drugs or selling for him in other clubs. Things that I most definitely did not want my baby sister doing. "What does Billy look like, Emily?"

"Kind of blond, with hair that covers his eyes. Really thin, but short for a guy." She hummed a bit into the phone as she thought it over. "Oh! He looks a lot like Bieber. But old."

"Old, huh? Are we talking thirty? Forty?"

Emily giggled, and I could imagine her holding a hand in front of her mouth. "I didn't say *ancient*, just old."

Well, I guess that made me old. At twenty-four, I'd never thought of myself that way before. Older, maybe, but never old. I guess when you were only seventeen or eighteen, anything with a two in front could seem pretty advanced.

I'd heard and even enjoyed some of the songs by Justin Bieber, but I had to really concentrate to remember what the kid looked like. I knew he had some of that medium length hair brushed across his forehead almost covering his eyes. Sounded like this Billy character grew it longer. I could remember thinking the kid looked almost androgynous, but that could be his age more than anything.

"You don't happen to know Billy's last name, do you?"

"Nuh uh," Emily said. "I don't think he ever said."

At least I had a place to start. With a name and description, I could go to this Shine place and hang out until I saw him. Or my sister. "Thank you for this, Emily. You have no idea how much you've helped me."

"I hope you find her, Jack. Jen is a great girl."

"She is," I agreed with a sad smile. It had just taken me too long to realize it. I pressed the button to end the call and groaned as I got to my feet. It would be hours until the club opened, and hours more before the crowds really started to arrive. I had to find something to do for the day, and the only thing I could think of was to keep driving around to see if I caught a glimpse of Jen. I felt more certain than ever now that I wouldn't see her, but it was better than sitting on the couch worrying myself into an early grave.

NOW

I retreated to my bed, hoping I could just forget about the last half hour and pretend it was nothing but a dream. Maybe it even was. I've had some very vivid dreams in my life, and this would be right in line with the kind of nightmares that loved to screw with my head.

I remembered one that happened a few years after my parents died. I was arguing with my dad about something stupid, the kind of inconsequential thing that you'd never argue about in real life, and I woke up irrationally angry with him. For most of the morning, I was so convinced dad was alive that I kept looking for him to continue our argument. Realizing the truth was like suffering the sucker punch of their loss all over again.

Tossing and turning for half an hour did nothing but get me even more worked up. What if Nyk's employer was right and the Magpie was still around? I'd been so certain that I put an end to the bastard ten years ago. If that wasn't the case, then I had no choice but to find the real Magpie and deal with them. I'd never be able to live with myself if I didn't.

Throwing off the covers, I groaned in frustration and padded into my small bathroom for a quick shower before throwing on reasonably clean clothes. Laundry day had come and gone yet again without me packing the full basket of dirty clothes to the laundromat several blocks away. One of these days, I'd get the plumbing fixed for the small room behind the kitchen built for the purpose.

I grabbed my gray herringbone coat from a hook by the door before walking into pre-dawn darkness. The air was filled with the cold, and I could feel my breath crystallizing when I exhaled. San Antonio was in for another morning below freezing, though it was supposed to be sunny and a little warmer by the afternoon.

As soon as I was in my car with the engine started, I turned on the seat warmers and cranked the heat up. I had to drive carefully on the short trip to my office building's parking lot. There were patches of ice on the roads, puddles from a brief shower the previous night that hadn't had time to evaporate. I felt the car jerk and slide a few times, but I managed to keep it on the road. Luckily, there weren't any other drivers around to worry about scraping against when my car veered into another lane before I got it back under control.

The ice proved a greater obstacle on my walk across the street after I parked in the deserted lot. I slipped a few times, landing flat on my back once when I stepped up onto the sidewalk in front of my building. As I lay there, staring up at the few stars I could see through the downtown light pollution, I could only be thankful that no one was around to see my embarrassment.

Snickering from a shadowy doorway nearby ruined that feeling. "That looks like it hurt, Dahlish," a creaky voice said. A face leaned out, the light from a streetlamp showing a greenish complexion with a wide smile that showed off teeth that were too sharp. The goblin was shaking with laughter, holding out a half empty bottle of cheap liquor as he pointed at me.

"Glad I could amuse you, Chip." I rose shakily to my feet, wiping at my coat to clear any dirt or grime from the street. Turning, I looked at the goblin and took a step closer. The small creature was huddled inside of a threadbare coat, with a filthy knit cap covering his few remaining strands of wiry black hair. Homeless Nox were a rarity, since the creatures tended to take responsibility for each other more than regular humans did, but Chip had been a creature of the streets for as long as I'd been aware of the supernatural world. I don't think anyone even knew what his real name was anymore.

I crouched down, wincing as I caught a whiff of cheap gin and unwashed body. "I hope you're not showing off that green face to others."

He laughed again, a croaking sound that was barely audible. "Only when they try to kick me." Chip took a deep drink of the swill in the glass bottle.

I could only sigh and shake my head as I stood up. "Don't make a habit of it, Chip. You know what I have to do if someone reports a green-skinned homeless guy." The goblin only held a hand in my direction, and I slipped a few bills into it. "Get down to the Y when it opens and get cleaned up. Okay?"

Pushing through the doors of my office building, I tried to put the goblin out of my mind. I'd spent a lot of time in my early years trying to get Chip settled in shelters or even set up with jobs. He would show up and behave for a few days, and then disappear and be back on the streets. I knew he preferred it there for some reason. Maybe it was a punishment for something in his past that he couldn't move beyond.

The lobby of the old Tower Life building was warm after the early morning cold, and I took a few seconds to enjoy it. A security guard was sitting behind a desk to the side, and he nodded when I looked in his direction. It was very rare for me to get to the office this early, but not at all uncommon for me to leave around midnight or later. I was one of the few who worked in the building that late, and the guards working the graveyard shift had come to recognize me.

With a wave, I passed into the marbled hallway where six elevators were located. As soon as I pressed a button there was an immediate ding and one of the doors slid open to emit bland elevator music. Background noise that I never normally noticed, but it proved incredibly irritating at five in the morning after a night of little sleep. I was already exhausted from a Saturday spent sanding floors, so a nearly sleepless night on top of that was proving to be a killer. When I'm tired, I get irritable and prickly.

It smelled a little stale when I walked into the first room of my small office suite, set up as a waiting room for clients. I hadn't been there in five days, and the scattered chairs and small tables were covered in a light film of dust. Okay, so that dust may have been there even when I was last in the office. I took a moment to straighten the handful of crinkled magazines on the low coffee table. The newest was already six months old, and I made a mental note to pick up some newer editions the next time I was in a store.

Just beyond the waiting area was the room set up as my personal sanctum. I had a small wooden desk in the middle of the room, mass produced but still nice enough to give an impression of someone doing well in their profession. To one side were a couple of heavy fireproof file cabinets, sturdy locks protecting the contents of the drawers. Mostly I kept my own hardcopy case notes from previous jobs there, to refer back to whenever I ran into similar situations or had to track down a Nox that wasn't among the most common breeds. On the other side was a storage closet. I'd paid to have a heavy steel door installed there, protecting items that I needed to hold onto and protect. Items that could prove to be incredibly dangerous in the wrong hands.

Behind the desk was my fancy swivel chair, a purchase that had set me back an arm and a leg. It was easily the most comfortable piece of furniture I owned, though. Sitting in the chair almost felt like floating on the surface of a placid lake, and I could spend hours there without feeling discomfort. I tossed my coat onto a wooden coatrack just inside the door before I plopped down in the chair to stare at my cluttered desk. My laptop was open, the screensaver cycling through some pictures of Ireland. I'd been wanting to take a vacation there for years, but I never had the time or money for it.

I thought about logging on and starting to search for information, but what would I even do? I don't think the services I had subscriptions for would return anything for a person called the Magpie. They tended to like full and proper names, maybe a social security number to really narrow it down. Aliases were almost impossible to track outside of the police department gang databases.

Instead, I turned my chair and looked through the large picture window that faced southeast. My view mostly consisted of the open-air parking lot where I always left my car, but I could see a portion of La Villita around the edge of a small office building on the far side of the lot. I could see the convention center and Tower of the Americas beyond that, over the roof of the office building. My office was high enough that I could see a lot of roofs, but not high enough to make it a great view.

The sky was starting to show a faint bit of light, and I think I kind of zoned out while I sat in the chair. I remember streaks of red and purple blossoming across the clouds, turning into orange and blue as the ball of fire that was our sun peeked over the horizon. I even remember dipping my head so that I wasn't staring directly into it. But the rest of the early morning was a blurry haze.

Falling asleep in a chair while I was supposed to be working. I was definitely turning into my dad. The man could sleep through a marching band in the living room.

When I looked at my phone, sitting on a wireless charging pad I bought after it went dead in a previous case and almost cost me my life, I was surprised to see it was already ten. Four hours gone to a waking doze instead of trying to track down information and leads. "Get it together, Dahlish," I said, running a hand over my face. Yeah, I talk to myself. Don't you?

After a trip to the restroom down the hall from my office, I grabbed my coat and phone and went back down the elevators.

There was one place I could think of that I might find answers about the Magpie, and it was only a half mile walk. The cold air would help to wake me up and invigorate my numb brain that was struggling to come up with any other ideas.

Chip was nowhere to be seen when I exited onto the street. I poked my head into a few places he could hole up for warmth, and I found them empty. Hopefully, he'd taken my advice about going to the YMCA. The little goblin could use the shower, and he might even find a hot meal if some of the folks who parked nearby and passed out supplies for the homeless were around.

Turning up the collar of my coat against the cold wind blowing in, I stuffed my hands into its pockets as I walked a few blocks to the first set of stairs leading down to the River-walk. The tourist destination was almost deserted at this time of the morning, only a few dozen hardy souls braving the cold to enjoy a Sunday morning walking along the still water.

My destination was only steps away from two very popular hotspots for tourists and locals alike, down five steps worn with years of usage until the middle of each was almost concave. The plain door was almost hidden, a growth of ivy climbing the walls all around. The name of the bar was hand painted in small letters beside the door, and I knew that most people passed by and never even looked at it. Those few who did would often have stories to share with friends at home, about the bar that felt a little off from the moment they stepped inside.

I pushed through the heavy door, letting it swing closed with a thump as I shrugged out of my coat and threw it across a stool. Sitting on the one beside it, I patted my hands on the comfortably worn and meticulously clean bar. The Lyon's Den was the only bar downtown where Nox could comfortably relax and not worry about having to keep up their human disguises. Once or twice a month, a ward would be erected to prevent errant tourists from entering and let the Nox hang out in all of their otherworldly glory.

"A little early for lunch," the bartender said, coming through a door that led into a small storage room behind the bar. Richard Lyon was also the owner of the bar, a human accepted and accepting of the supernatural Filii Nox. Richard was in possession of a Relic, imbued with the chaotic energies that first formed the universe and created the gods who had given birth to the first generations of Filii Nox. Not that he ever mentioned it. I didn't even know what it was, only that I could feel it tugging at my senses when he was close.

"I was hoping for something more along the information variety," I told him, reaching up to stroke the amulet always around my neck. It was a silver coin pierced by a chain that never seemed to tarnish or collect dirt no matter where I wore it. The face on both sides of the coin was a profile in gold that no historian had ever been able to identify, surrounded by a script that matched nothing known to exist. I'd worn the talisman for a decade, and still knew just as much about it as I had the moment I put it around my neck.

"What kind of information are you looking for this time, Jack?" Richard was wiping a clean rag over the bar top, whether habit or OCD I could never tell. His medium length brown hair was tied back today, though he usually let it fall wherever it may.

I took a deep breath and let it out as a long sigh. "The Magpie. I killed him. Didn't I, Richard?"

He didn't answer, meeting my eyes for a moment before turning away. The silence stretched out, broken only by the sound of glass clinking against the metal tap. Dark brown liquid poured out, leaving an inch of foam reaching the lip of the glass when it was pulled away from the tap. Richard set it in front of me, leaning both hands on the bar.

"A little early for a drink, isn't it?" I asked. Habit made me reach out and pick up the glass to take a sip. There was a hint of blackberries once I swallowed, and I wondered which local microbrewery had produced it.

"I've been hearing some stories for a while," Richard said, slowly. "A few years, actually. Stories that there was someone out there looking to buy anything related to the Nox. I've seen people come in here with a stack of cash but missing random things." He looked up and met my eye, and I could see sorrow there. "I had a feeling, but I was never sure, Jack. I didn't want to say anything until I was."

Cursing, I lay my head on my arms. "It doesn't have to be the Magpie. Maybe someone else decided to fill the role. Start collecting a bunch of nonsensical things that have no real value."

"Someone was in here about a month ago, offering to buy a certain possession of mine." I could hear the caution in his voice, the habitual reluctance to admit he had a Relic.

36

I lifted my head, remembering the night I'd seen him deep in conversation with two people on the far end of the bar. That had been during the case of the kidnapped kids, when Penny's grandmother hired me to find her. Richard seemed to read my thoughts from the direction of my gaze, and he nodded. "How much did they offer?" I asked, more curiosity than anything.

"A lot," he said with a snort. "Enough that I'd never have to worry about cost again when I wanted to get something for this place. Hell, enough to buy a hundred other bars across the country, turn them into havens for the Nox, and never have to worry about cost when I need to buy anything for them."

"That's a lot of money." I admit that I wondered for a few moments how much they'd offer for my own Relic. In fact, I felt a little offended they'd never asked to buy it. "At the same time, there aren't many people with such deep pockets."

"No, there's not."

"Shit." I couldn't keep kidding myself now. Magpie was the only person who'd ever thrown that kind of money at the Nox community. Sure, a lot of the families had built up piles of wealth over the centuries that weren't frittered away as human heirs often would, but none of that came close to the kind of money Richard was talking about. "How did they even know you had something they'd want to buy?"

Richard shook his head. "I tried to get them to tell me that, without admitting that I had anything they'd be interested in. They were positive about it, though. The only people who should know it are the Nine." I grunted at that, surprised that the bartender knew my amulet and the eight others like it gave the ability to sense Relics. But then, Richard was the one who filled me in on a lot of what the talisman was capable of when I found myself in possession of it.

"Double shit." The Magpie was still out there, and now I had to track him down all over again.

THEN

It was my third night in a row at Shine, sitting at a table in a corner of the noisy club with an outrageously overpriced drink that I was sipping as slowly as possible. Any time the glass was empty, the circulating bouncers started to give me the stink eye until I ordered a new one. My rapidly dwindling savings account wouldn't allow me to spend much more time in my search for Billy. Especially if I kept dragging through my work from lack of sleep and got fired.

On the first night, I'd mingled among the groups of men and women in the club. I'd join in for some small talk before asking if they knew where Billy was, trying to make it sound like he was someone I knew. I got a few side-eye glances, but no one would claim to know him or when he'd be at Shine again. By the second night, anyone who recognized me from the previous evening would turn away whenever I approached.

A waitress passed by my table, carrying a few empty glasses on a tray. She squinted her eyes at my half full beer, which I'd ordered an hour before. I took a sip to show her I was still drinking it, but kept my eyes roving across the crowd. I continued hoping to see a mop of blond hair that would prove to be the elusive drug dealer, but it was such a popular hair style in the club that I'd often chase someone across the room only to find it was the last guy I'd looked at.

I felt a presence behind me after a while, and I slowly turned my head to see a large white guy less than a foot away. He was a few inches shorter than my six feet, but wide enough for two of me. Some of it was fat, but most of it was clearly muscle judging by the bulging arms under his sky-blue button up shirt. The top button couldn't even be closed around his thick neck. Several tattoos were visible at his wrists and on his neck, and his hair was shaved on the sides to form a kind of trimmed hedge mohawk on top and back. The sunglasses covering his eyes seemed unnecessary inside the dim club.

"Can I help you?" I asked, trying not to show how intimidated I felt.

"Boss wants to see you," he said, his lips barely moving as he spoke. A meaty hand was held out to indicate the direction he wanted me to go.

"Uh, no thanks?" I held up my half empty glass of beer. "I'm heading out as soon as I finish this drink. Big day at work tomorrow, and all that."

"Boss wants to see you," he said again, in exactly the same tone. His hand was still held up.

I sighed, took a swallow of the beer to cure my suddenly dry mouth, and then slid off the chair. The crowd seemed to part before us as I was ushered toward the rear of the club, and more than one of the partiers gave me pitying looks as I passed. "So, Moses, where are we going?" I asked, trying to cover my fear with humor.

"Boss wants to see you," he repeated. Yep, same tone and everything.

"Yeah, yeah. The boss." I muttered as we approached a door guarded by another bouncer. He nodded once at the man behind me, then reached out to knock twice on the door. Within seconds it was opened by a third bouncer. A gentle shove between my shoulder blades propelled me into the short, dark hallway beyond. There was a door on either side, but I was guided to the one at the end.

A beefy arm reached past me to knock on the door, a more complicated rhythm of two loud knocks followed by three gentle taps and one last heavy thump. I looked up and saw a camera pointed at me above the door, fighting back an irrational temptation to wave and make faces. When the door opened, I was especially glad I'd resisted. In addition to the black-suited muscle holding the door, two more were seated on a leather couch to the side. One of them was a woman, and I could almost feel her eyes burning into me from behind her sunglasses. A brief thought flitted across my brain that she was the most dangerous person in the room, despite the obvious brawn of the men.

Behind the desk was a thin guy, almost reedy looking with wrists so narrow they seemed like they would break if he tried to do a push up. His lips were pulled up in a snarky grin, and his eyes were obscured by the fringe of his dishwater blonde hair swept across his forehead.

"Well, well, well," the kid said. "This is the guy that's been tossing my name out left and right the last few nights?"

"Yeah, boss," the bouncer behind me rumbled. I jumped, not realizing he'd followed me into the tight office.

"Are you Billy?" I asked, stepping forward in an attempt at showing I wasn't afraid of the four very imposing and scary people in the room with us.

He turned his grin toward me, chuckling. "Yeah, genius. I'm Billy. To my friends. Losers like you call me Mr. Wish."

Billy Wish? What the hell kind of name was that? "Look, I'm not here to cause any trouble. I'm looking for my sister, and I heard she might be with you." I reached into a back pocket for my wallet, pausing for a moment when I saw the bodyguards around me tense up at the movement. I moved more slowly, pulling a picture from my wallet to hold up. "Her name is Jen. Jennifer Dahlish. Please tell me you know where she is."

He never even looked at the picture, just looked past me to the two suited guards on the couch as he shook his head and laughed. "Can you believe this guy? What am I, a babysitter?"

"She's nineteen, and I know she met you in this club a month ago. Her friends say she went out with you a week later, maybe more than once."

A heavy hand landed on my shoulder, turning me to face the bouncer who escorted me into the room. His tattooed hand pulled the photo from my fingers and balled it up as I cried out in shock. "Listen up, loser," Billy said from behind the desk, where he'd propped feet encased in overly large shiny black boots. "I meet a lot of chicks in this place, and they all want something from me. Maybe one of them was your sister, maybe not. I don't look at faces too much, if you know what I mean." He let out a braying laugh, looking around at his bodyguards. None of them smiled.

"You spent a couple of hours talking with her," I insisted, frowning at the bouncer as I picked up the picture of my sister. It had been creased and torn in his hands, and I smoothed it out as best I could. "Look, I'm not asking what you and she did on your dates. I just want to know she's safe, and not dealing drugs for you or something."

Billy focused his attention on me for the first time, sliding his feet off the desk as he sat up and leaned forward. "What did you just say, douchebag? What makes you think I'm some low-life drug dealer?"

The suddenly calm seriousness of his tone freaked me out, maybe more than all four heads of the bouncer and bodyguards turning to look at me. "One of her friends saw you passing pa-per packets to people," I said with a lame shrug. "What else could it be?"

He stared at me in silence for half a minute, his eyes almost bulging out of the sockets. Suddenly, he slapped a hand on the desk, making me jump. Breaking out in his braying laughter, Billy leaned back in the chair again. "This guy," he said to the bodyguards, waving a hand in my direction. "I didn't think he could get more pathetic, but he keeps opening his mouth and proving me wrong."

Turning back to me, he held a finger up to the side of his head. "Do you have the brain cells to understand that drugs are not the only thing worth selling? What I provide is much more than a simple chemical high. I give people access to things they've never imagined before. A taste of power that your puny little brain couldn't even begin to grasp."

43

I had no idea what he was going on about, but with the focus back on the kid, I was able to take three quick steps to lean on the desk. "Please! Billy…Mr. Wish, please just tell me my sister is okay. I'll never bother you again."

A tree trunk arm wrapped around my midsection, pulling me roughly from the desk. I'd seen a brief flash of fear in the kid's eyes as I got close to him, but now he was back to his dismissive attitude. "Oh, you ain't gonna bother me again. That's for sure, loser." He snapped his fingers and pointed at me with two fingers. "Take this crazy idiot out back and show him what'll happen if he comes back here."

I struggled against the bouncer, but I might as well have been fighting a brick wall for all the good it did. He finally grabbed one of my hands in a crushing grip and twisted my arm behind my back hard enough to make me yelp with pain. I couldn't move without making it hurt worse, and he marched me back to the hallway.

The bouncer there was holding another door open halfway down the hall, and I was propelled through it into a filthy alley. I could see the main road at the far end, but we were at least fifty feet away. Two large dumpsters blocked us from view of anyone passing by the mouth of the alley, and the bouncer shoved me against the concrete block wall. A meaty hand was placed on my chest to keep me there as the three bodyguards filed out the door.

"Drugs? Is that seriously what you thought was going on here?" the woman asked, stepping close enough that I could feel her stale breath on my cheek. She was half a foot shorter than me, but I felt incredibly intimidated. More so when I happened to see the butt of a pistol in a shoulder harness as her jacket flapped in a light breeze.

I gulped and had to work spit into my mouth before I could make words. "Guys, I don't care what's going on. I just want to find my sister. Don't you have sisters you'd do the same for? Or brothers?"

Not one of them moved, except for the woman who shook her head and pulled the sunglasses from her face. Two dark eyes bored holes into mine. "Billy should have remembered her. I recognize the girl from your picture. Cute little thing, with her purple hair."

I gasped at that, since the picture I'd shown them was of Jen with her natural brown. "Where is she? Please, just tell me."

"She's with us now," the woman said, almost sadly. "That's all you need to know. That's all you'll *ever* know." She tilted her head and looked into my eyes. "But you're not going to be satisfied with that, are you? I see fear in your eyes, Mr. Dahlish, but I also see determination buried behind it. Pity."

The woman stepped back, glancing to one of the muscle-bound cretins in a suit. She was almost a blur as she spun around and slammed a foot into my stomach. I coughed out all the air in my lungs. It seemed ages before I was able to suck in a gasping breath. The pain in my wrist and shoulder were forgotten. My stomach was forgotten soon after, when an almost dainty fist smacked into my jaw. The uppercut snapped my head back to bounce against the concrete wall.

Stars were swimming in my eyes as a large hand gripped the back of my neck and almost tossed me across the narrow alley to slam into the opposite wall. Before I could get my balance back, a foot swept my legs out from beneath me. I landed face first on the hard asphalt and heard a crunch as my nose impacted. Blood was pouring out as another hand grabbed my hair and forced me up onto my knees.

The woman pressed her face close to mine, eyes shining with excitement and anticipation. I got the feeling she was enjoying beating the crap out of me way more than I was. "Are you listening, moron? Don't. Fuck. With. The Magpie."

"Please," I tried to say through the pain and blood. "Stop."

A fist harder than stone slammed into my stomach. Once, twice, three times. While I was trying to convince my body to breathe again, a knee slammed into my face and threw me onto my back. Heavy shoes began to kick at me then, as I tried to roll into a ball and protect myself. I heard snaps as a few ribs cracked, and I was trying to work up the breath to scream for help when one of the shoes hit my temple.

NOW

It was close to noon when I walked back into my office, carrying a small white business card Richard had been given by the two people making the offer to buy his Relic. It was made from a heavy cardstock, the kind you could rub your finger across and instantly recognize as expensive. My own cards looked incredibly shabby in comparison. I had one plain white card with just my name and cell number, and a light gray card that I handed out most often showing my name, phone number, email address, and private detective license number. I'd bought a box of five hundred of each card for less than twenty bucks. That much cash might have bought a dozen like the card I now held in my hand.

The only thing on the white card was a phone number. It was local, with a 210 area code. The first thing I did was try to call it. Leaning back in my chair, I turned to look through the window as I held my phone to my ear and listened to the ring. After twenty seconds, it was still ringing. I canceled the call and swiveled back to my desk to log on to my laptop. Several of the sites I had paid memberships for gave me tools to look up information on phone numbers, as well as addresses, social security numbers, names, and a dozen other things that I used to help me find people I was tracking down.

Within five minutes, I was staring at the results of my search. The problem was that the three sites I'd started a search on all returned different results. One said the number belonged to a retirement home on the south side of town, an establishment that no longer existed according to Google. The second search said the number would reach a pawn shop on the near west side, another business that Google couldn't find. The last search claimed it was for a costume shop on the north side of town. It had apparently closed down a decade ago, another victim of the recession.

I leaned back and tried to conjure up my memories of what the two people in the bar had looked like. I'd been in the early stages of the case with the missing kids back then, still thinking Penny was the only one I was looking for. I was at the Den, waiting for Ollie to arrive; he's a sergeant with the SAPD, and the only cop I was sure knew about the Nox. Richard had been at the far end of the bar, leaning in to talk with two people. The man had been closest to me, though that was still thirty feet away. He was average height and his profile had been strong, with a sharp jawline and nose that could chisel icebergs. It had been hard to tell in the dim lighting, but I thought his hair was blonde or light brown, swept back from his forehead and held in place with far too much hairspray or mousse.

The woman had been mostly obscured by him. She was a few inches shorter, and estimating from Richard's height across the bar I'd put her at about five and a half feet. Black hair, shoulder length from the way it fell forward when she looked down to pull out the white card and hand it to the bartender.

I tried to remember more about them, but it had been so dark in the bar and I had been focused on another case. I'd only

48

noticed them as a curiosity, because of the way Richard seemed slightly uncomfortable as he talked to them. My intention had been to ask about them the next time I was at the Den, but it had left my mind the moment I was out the door and chasing the next lead on my case.

One thing did suddenly come to me, though. Something that had struck me as odd in the moment but wasn't terribly uncommon among the Nox. The woman had been wearing sunglasses in the dim bar. Some varieties of the supernatural had strange eyes that they couldn't disguise with their human faces, so sunglasses had become an accepted method. Pupils that had a slight glow or formed odd shapes that were hard to explain to your average human.

I felt the air leave my body as if I'd been punched. I held an arm over my ribs, remembering the beating I'd taken in the alley so many years ago. Those bodyguards had worn dark suits and sunglasses, which at the time had struck me as such a cliché. After all, it was the kind of thing you saw in TV shows and movies all the time. You never expected to see it in real life. It had been an effective cliché, though, since I'd felt a spike of fear the moment I saw them in that office at the back of the club.

Unless the two people at the bar had been with the Secret Service, that made it even more convincing that Magpie was still around. I was feeling more like a failure now. As I had in the week I was stuck in the hospital after the beating. Wondering if I could work up the courage to go back to the club and look for my sister again. Back then, I'd given up and admitted defeat.

I was a different person now, and it would take a lot more to force me to back down. If I screwed up something this important ten years ago, there was nothing that would keep me from making it right. I grabbed my cell phone again, scrolling through the Contacts list and selecting a number to dial.

"Nyk, I'm in."

The bounty hunter arrived forty minutes later, carrying two bags filled with burgers and fries. The smaller one that he passed to me had a single burger and small fries, while his large bag had the same thing times three. I was ravenous after skipping breakfast and only drinking a few sips of the beer at the Den, so I ripped open the bag and took a huge bite of the burger. It was only slightly warm after the long drive from the burger place on Loop 410, but that didn't bother me at all. One bite was all it took to bring great memories of a redheaded reporter flooding back.

Nyk somehow inhaled his three burgers before I'd finished my one, and he was licking his fingers clean as I shook my head in wonder. As I chewed my last bites, I filled him in on the two people in the Lyon's Den. He looked at the card, flipping it over a few times as if looking for hidden information somewhere. "Magpie," he said, simply.

"Huh?"

"Same kinds of cards were circulating a decade ago. Any Nox that seemed down on their luck would be approached and told to call the number if they wanted to make some money. I was even passed a card once, by a client who told me I could get triple my usual fee if I wanted to do some work that might not be exactly legal."

"Holy hells! Did you ever call?"

Nyk raised an eyebrow as he looked at me. "Of course not. I knew that meant kidnapping or roughing up poor Nox just trying to stay on the up and up. I may be a bounty hunter, but I have my principles. Same as you, Jack."

I raised my hands in surrender. "I didn't think you'd really take a job like that. I'm just curious if that number gave a response of any kind."

"Why?" He looked down at the card, and then back to me. "Please tell me you didn't call this number, Jack."

Shrugging, I pointed at my phone. "I called, but no one ever answered. It just rings and rings."

Nyk shook his head and gave an exasperated sigh. He started to ball up the empty wrappers and bags from our meal. "They'll know you're looking now. If you were going to do something that boneheaded, you should have at least used a phone that couldn't be traced back to you." He stood and crossed to throw the debris in the trash can I kept in the waiting room.

"I had to call!" I said in protest. "That number is our only real lead. It's not like the trace pulled anything helpful."

"That costume shop, that's a lead."

"The place has been closed for ten years. How are we going to get anything from that?"

Nyk snorted and one side of his mouth pulled up in a smirk. "What else happened ten years ago, Mr. Investigator? Something that occurred around the same time?"

I looked at him in total confusion. "Pretty sure the recession has nothing to do with some shadowy underworld figure preying on the Nox community."

Look, I'll admit it. My brain is a bit slow sometimes. I get focused on something, and I don't take the time to process anything outside of that narrow stream of information. To my credit, the light did finally dawn. "Wait... I took down the person I thought was the Magpie that year. You think they could be related?"

"Only one way to find out, right?" Nyk grabbed my coat from the rack and tossed it to me. "We can check out the other two address, as well. The businesses don't exist anymore, but maybe what's really there will give us some clues."

Riding down in the elevator with the hulking giant was a real experience. I suddenly understood how sardines felt stuffed into a tin can. We stopped twice on the way to the lobby. Both times the person waiting took one look at Nyk and politely told us they'd wait for the next one. I was tempted to jump off and wait with them.

Passing through the lobby, I pulled on my coat and patted my pockets to make sure I still had my keys. I really don't know why I always did that, when I never pulled them out of my pocket for anything through the day. "I'll drive."

"Nah, we're taking mine." I said a silent prayer in thanks for that. I really didn't know how the bounty hunter was going to fit in my tiny little Honda. He led me along the street for half a block to where he'd parked by a meter. The truck was just as large as Nyk was, one of those crew cab models with a second row of full seating and doubled up rear wheels that extended the width of the vehicle. On top of all that, I knew he'd thrown a lot of money into custom work to build a stronger frame. When you got paid to track down people who didn't want to be found, it wasn't uncommon to end up in a chase along back roads full of ruts and bumps. Or to get shot at, which the thicker door panels and bulletproof glass would help with.

Sliding into the passenger seat, I almost felt like a kid again. I had twice as much leg room as in my car, and the seat was wider and deeper. The leather was also as soft as a newborn baby, and I was stroking my hand along the seat for several seconds before I realized what I was doing.

Nyk started the truck, a throaty growl that probably shook the nearby buildings and made people wonder if Texas had earthquakes now. He pressed down on the clutch and shifted into gear smoothly, a feat I was truly impressed with. I'd taken a few lessons on a manual transmission as a kid, and I'm sure I stripped those gears to nubs by the time I was done. My dad had chuckled and told me to stick to automatic in future.

Nyk didn't even look as he pulled away from the curb, accelerating into the flow of traffic amid a few horns from irate drivers. I looked over warily, but he only shrugged. "When you drive the closest thing to a tank, other people pay attention to you. Not the other way around."

"Uh huh," I said. This was my first time going anywhere with him, and I wasn't feeling very confident that it would be repeated in future. "You know you just missed the turn to go back to 281 North."

"We'll check the address for the retirement home on the south side first. No point in having to backtrack later on. It's only a mile from here."

I looked around the dash. "Where's your GPS? Do you need me to pull up directions?" One of my few splurges when I bought a newer car six years ago was paying extra for one with satellite navigation. You would be surprised how many times I had to rely on the gizmo to tell me how to get to an address I'd uncovered. Or to get back home when I'd finally found it.

Nyk only laughed, a thundering sound that seemed to vibrate the truck as much as the engine did. "Jack, I've been driving around this city for a dozen years. I don't need maps or computer voices telling me where to go."

He proved it in less than ten minutes, pulling up to the curb beside the address listed for the retirement home without one single wrong turn. I stared through the windshield at the empty lot across the cracked and potholed pavement. "Well, that's definitely not a retirement home."

"Not now, but check your fancy phone and see if you can find out what was there ten years ago."

I almost smacked my forehead. It was something I should have thought to do without the prompting. I logged onto one of my property record apps, plugged in the address, and requested any historical information. Then I stared at a spinning circle for several minute as the database chugged away on my request.

"Okay," I said, once the results came up. "Looks like this address really was a retirement home, listed as belonging to a company called Pica Sericea beginning in 1973. Registered ownership is some island in the Pacific I've never heard of."

"Shell corporation."

"Oh yeah, big time. Sold to a property developer six years ago, but I guess they haven't had a chance to do anything with it yet. Other than tear down the old building." I kept scrolling through the tiny print on the screen, squinting as I looked for anything relevant to our search. "Before '73, it looks like there was some kind of restaurant here. It gets pretty muddy the farther back you go on property records, though. Lots of breaking up parcels to sell off in smaller chunks."

"So, the retirement home was here ten years ago? Was it still open, with people living there?"

I did a few other searches, first Google and then the city records. "Ah. It was shut down in 2013, due to cases of neglect and patients dying from unexplained causes. Those complaints started around 2010. Fall."

Nyk grunted, thinking the same thing I did about that information. Without a word, he shifted and pulled into the street again. We were headed west, to the location of the pawn shop listed under the phone number. As he drove, I started doing property searches for that address.

"Weird. This address was owned by a company called Pica Hudsonia, starting in 1974. That company is registered in

55

Mauretania. The pawn shop is still there, but apparently it was bought out by some big national chain in 2014. Same month that the retirement home was sold."

A few minutes later we pulled into the parking lot. The large sign out front looked fairly new, with giant white letters on a blue background. The pole it was attached to had the look of something added when the property changed hands, making me think the previous owners weren't too interested in advertising.

"What's Pica?" Nyk asked softly. "Sounds familiar, and both companies have that in the name."

"Probably some family name," I said with a shrug. "Let's see what the all-knowing internet has to say. Uh...it's an eating disorder? Oh! That's the thing where people will eat all kinds of weird junk like glass or hair. So gross." I went through several pages of results, all about the eating disorder, before modifying the search. "But Pica Hudsonia..."

I flipped the phone and held it so Nyk could see the screen. He grimaced, looking at the picture of the little black and white bird, a species known as the American Magpie. I then looked up the first company's name, revealing an image of a species known as the Oriental Magpie.

The address of the third location turned out to have been owned by a company called Cissa Hypoleuca. A search of that showed the Indochine Magpie, a colorful species of blue and green bird with red wing tips. The costume shop closed in 2010, but the property was not sold off until six years ago when a neighboring strip mall purchased it to expand their footprint.

Fifteen minutes later, we were parked nearby staring at a discount clothing chain occupying the newly renovated location.

"Shit," I said, staring down at the picture of the latest bird. "Every one of them was tied to the Magpie."

"But they were all sold off in 2014," Nyk said. "With the businesses closing or going quickly downhill after 2010. I have to tell you, Jack, if not for my employer and that business card your bartender friend gave you, I'd be convinced you really did take down the Magpie back then."

"At least I hurt the bastard. It just took him ten years to climb his way back up." I sighed and ran my fingers through my hair, watching a rather rotund middle-aged woman push through the doors of the clothing store carrying three stuffed bags. "Where do we go from here? The phone number only led us to businesses that aren't even owned by him any longer."

That's when my cell phone began to ring. I looked down at it in surprise, seeing BLOCKED on the caller ID display. It rang three times while I stared at it, until finally Nyk nudged me and motioned that I should answer. I did, putting it on speaker. "Hello?"

"Mr. Dahlish, I do apologize for not answering when you called this morning." The voice was garbled, electronically altered so that I couldn't tell if it were a male or female. There was a touch of an accent, something that was almost Eastern European. "My employer has instructed me to congratulate you on tracing three of the properties that used to belong to us. They were a very small part of a vast empire, which I assure you is still alive and well to this day. As is my employer."

"Let me talk to the Magpie," I said. My fingers were gripping the phone so hard I heard the case creak in protest.

"My employer is sadly unavailable at this moment, but I have been instructed to pass on a gentle warning. Remember the alley and the pond, Mr. Dahlish, lest history repeat itself in a way you are not prepared to handle."

"Oh, and Mr. Walsh," the voice continued, dripping with sarcasm as it spoke Nyk's last name. A name that I knew to be adopted to protect whatever past he had before coming to Texas. "My employer would have me caution you against providing any further assistance to Mr. Dahlish. We know who hired you, and your services will no longer be required."

A click filled the silent cab of the truck as the line disconnected. I could see Nyk glaring at the phone, something in his eyes I'd never seen before. Hesitation.

Making a quick decision, I pried off the back of my phone's case. I pulled the battery, having to yank hard to separate the wires that connected it to the system board. Next, I ejected the SIM card, snapped it in half, and then rolled down the window to toss all of it to the pavement. "Let's go," I said, still seething from the casual contempt in the tone of whatever lackey had spoken to us. "And stop at a store somewhere so I can buy a new phone."

THEN

Blinking my eyes open, I could see only white. I squinted against the light and tried to raise a hand to shield my eyes. My arm was heavy for some reason, and as I tried harder to move it, I groaned at the pain that shot through my body. I turned my head away from the light, blinking as I waited for my eyes to adjust so I could see.

"Mr. Dahlish?"

The voice wasn't far away, but I couldn't see where it came from. I heard a swishing sound, and suddenly the amount of light dropped. Footsteps circled the bed, and a woman's face appeared above me.

"Is that better, Mr. Dahlish?"

"Yeah," I said. Or at least I tried to. My mouth was so dry that an incoherent croak was the best I could do. I heard liquid splashing into a cup, and then felt a plastic straw against my lips. I sucked at the water as much as I could. More of it seemed to drip down my cheek than my throat, but it was enough to get rid of the gummy feeling. "Yeah," I said again. "Thank you."

"I'll let the doctor know that you're awake. We've been worried about you, sir."

"Where am I?" That's what I was trying to say, anyway. My head was starting to feel fuzzy, and I'm not entirely sure how many syllables I fit the words into.

"You're at Saint David's, Mr. Dahlish. Do you remember what happened to you?"

I got hit by a truck. Make that four trucks. If it weren't too much effort, I would have said the words aloud.

It took a while for my brain to catch up to the woman's words. Saint David's? There was no Saint David's hospital in San Antonio. I could see now that the woman leaning over me was wearing scrubs. She had to be a nurse since she said she'd call the doctor. "Austin?" I asked.

"Yes, St. David's in Austin." Her face was still out of focus, but I could see her brows draw together. Probably thinking I was a loon. "You were found outside the emergency room two nights ago. Do you remember what happened to you?"

Why would the bodyguards beat me half to death, and then drive me an hour north to dump me at a hospital? There were tons of hospitals in San Antonio. Very good ones, too. The fact that I'd been there for two days was starting to sink in when a man in a white coat swept into the room with his nose buried in my charts. I must have gotten lost in my thoughts for longer than I realized, since the nurse was nowhere to be seen.

"Mr. Dahlish, it's good to see you awake," the doctor said, finally looking up at me. Without warning, a small flashlight shone into my eyes. I was left blinded again when it was pulled away, and felt the covers lifted as the doctor examined me. "It's always tricky with concussions as bad as the one you suffered. Your pupils aren't as responsive as I like, so I'll order another MRI for you."

"How bad?" I asked.

I must have been coherent enough for the doctor to understand me, as he placed a hand on my shoulder and met my eyes. "You've got a broken arm that will be in a cast for at least a month, three broken ribs that will need time to heal, a tear in your shoulder muscle that might require surgery, and more bruises than I've seen in a lot of car accident victims. There was some minor internal bleeding, but we got that fixed up nicely. I imagine you can't feel much of it right now, with the amount of morphine we're pumping into you."

He kept chattering on in a pleasant voice, telling me about treatment plans and physical therapy, but I closed my eyes and shut him out. I could feel trails of moisture rolling from my eyes as I thought about Jennifer. What kind of situation had she found herself in, if this is how I got treated just for asking about her? I felt more certain than ever that I needed to find her.

At the same time, I didn't think I had the courage to face another beating. For the sake of my own life, I would have to forget about my sister and let her get in touch with me when she felt like it. *If* she ever felt like it.

By the time I was released from St David's, I'd been stuck in the hospital for six days. It wasn't until the third that I was able to stay awake for more than an hour. On the fourth I could actually start to hold a normal conversation without losing track of my words halfway through. The doctor kept me a bit longer just to make sure everything in my head was healing as it should.

The hospital bill I was shown while signing all the paperwork for my release almost made me pass out. It was more than I could hope to make in a year. Two years, even, unless I got some fabulous promotion. And that wasn't likely since the bank had left messages on my phone that I was being let go for too many unexplained absences. I tried to call my boss and explain about being unconscious in the hospital, but he just spouted off company policies and said the matter was out of his hands.

So I found myself sitting on a bench by the curb outside the hospital without a job or any prospects, an hour away from home, and no closer to my sister than I had been the day I found her note. As the sun set and night descended around me, I had to sit there with only myself for company. Knowing that I lacked the courage to go any further in my search.

It was very late when a sputtering old car pulled up at the curb, and a loud honk dragged me from my thoughts. When I found out I was being released from the hospital, I'd called up one of my old college friends who was willing to pick me up after work.

"Jesus, Jack, you look like hell. Did you get hit by a Mack truck?" I'd been unable to pull my blood-stained t-shirt on over the cast, so I was sitting there in just blue jeans. My chest was still wrapped in compression bandages for my healing ribs, and vivid purple bruises covered almost every inch of my exposed skin. I groaned as I pushed myself to unsteady feet. The morphine had been withdrawn the day before, and the codeine tablet I had taken with lunch had mostly worn off.

62

"I think I would have preferred the truck," I said, as Eddie got out of the car and circled to hold the passenger door open for me. "At least the truck wouldn't have kept hitting me." He had to help me lower myself into the car, and I winced as I settled into the seat. Every bruise ached at the contact. It was going to be a week before I could sit comfortably, at the least.

"You should've called sooner, dude." Eddie said as he slid behind the wheel. "I would have come to visit you."

"I didn't even know where I was until a few days ago. They told me, but it wasn't getting through to my memory."

He cast a side-eye glance at me as the car coasted toward a red light. "Seriously, Jack. What the hell happened? What kind of trouble did you get yourself into?"

Sighing, I told him about my sister leaving. Eddie had met her a few times when he dropped by my apartment. He didn't seem as shocked as I had hoped when I told him she left, but he did squeeze my shoulder in sympathy. Then I told him about the call from Emily, and her information about Billy.

"Duuude," he said, drawing the word out. "I wish you would've called me. Shine is not the kind of club for you and me. I've heard stories about that place."

"What kind of stories? Drugs?"

"No, man, in fact I've heard it's totally clean. Won't let the usual dealers in at all, and if you get caught carrying you get a lifetime ban from entering." Eddie drove in silence for a bit, coasting along the overpass that put us onto I-35 going south to home. "What I heard is that it's a place for the freaks and geeks crowd to hang out. Like, super freaky and geeky."

I thought back to the people I'd seen during my three nights in the club. None of them had seemed out of the ordinary, though I was mostly occupied with searching the crowd for my sister or Billy. If anything, they'd seemed more vibrant than the crowds I usually found myself among at bars or clubs. More alive. It felt good to know the club was hard set against drugs, but then I just started worrying about what they were selling instead.

"So how does going into the freak club end with you in a cast and wrapped up like a mummy?"

"Club management disagreed with my presence," I said, trying to decide how much I wanted to tell him. For some reason, I was reluctant to mention the bodyguards and anything discussed in the office or alley. "I did accuse him of dealing drugs."

"Dude! You don't just say something like that straight out. Doesn't justify that much of a beating, though."

I almost shrugged, and then remembered the spike of pain I felt every time I moved the shoulder of my broken arm. The muscles there were still repairing from when the bouncer and forced my arm behind my back and kept putting more pressure on it. It was my right arm, so I'd be learning how to do things left-handed until the cast came off. My wrist had been snapped, and the awkward position of the cast kept my thumb from moving enough to touch any fingers. It itched like crazy, too.

Eddie was looking at me now and then, his gaze calculating as he took in all the bruises and wrappings. "How many guys jumped you? No way only one person did that much damage."

"It was four," I groaned, leaning back gingerly on the head-rest. "The lady did most of it, though, from what I remember."

"Lady?!" That's when I realized I'd made a mistake, as Eddie burst out laughing. He was shaking so hard the car was almost bouncing, slapping at the wheel with mirth. "Jack got beat up by a lady! See what happens when you go out without your wingman?"

"To be fair, she had three huge guys backing her up. Pretty sure they did a good amount of the hitting and kicking."

Eddie kept laughing off and on for the rest of the drive, and I knew I was going to be hearing the story about getting beat up by a girl for years to come. At least I'd be able to laugh about it once the cast and bruises were gone. I wasn't sure I'd feel the same way about my inability to generate the courage needed to keep searching for my sister.

We went through a drive-thru for some tacos and soda, and then Eddie dropped me off outside my apartment. He helped me get out of the car and into the apartment, squinting at me as I struggled to open the small sample packet of pain killers the nurse had given me earlier in the day. "Are you going to be okay on your own, dude?"

"Yeah, I'll be fine." I waved at him to leave as I chewed on the pills to make them work faster. "These things will put me to sleep in half an hour. It's not like I'm crippled, Eddie, just beat to shit."

He stuck around for a few more minutes, hovering like a worried mother hen. "I'm going to call and check on you tomorrow. You need me to take you somewhere after work? Pharmacy or something?"

"Well, I do need to get my car. If it's still in the lot I parked it in before going into Shine."

"Dude. Your car has been parked in the warehouse district for a week, and you think it's still there?" He was smiling now, shaking his head in disbelief. "If it didn't get towed, it probably ended up in a chop shop somewhere."

That's exactly what I was afraid of, but I didn't have the mental bandwidth to deal with it right then. I could already feel the fuzziness clouding my mind as the pain killers took hold.

"Look," Eddie said, standing with a hand on the doorknob to leave the apartment. "I'll drive by before work in the morning. See if there's a crappy old Buick sitting in the lot." He smiled as he left, and I raised my good arm in a halfhearted wave.

My car wasn't in the lot. It also wasn't at the impound when I called to ask about it. So now, on top of not having a job or any savings left, with huge hospital bills looming, I had no transportation. A couple of uniformed cops came by and took a report for the theft, but I could tell from their glances they were convinced I wasn't being entirely truthful. One of them asked me point blank if I got beat up during a carjacking. I wasn't about to tell them what really happened and risk Billy sending his goons after me again, so I said it was a mugging and left it at that.

Two weeks later, there had been no sign of my car. My insurance company had been unhelpful, pointing out that by paying the bare minimum for liability insurance the theft wasn't covered. I called the police department every day to ask for an update, and I could hear the person on the phone lose interest once they pulled up the details and saw the age and make of the car. Their tone of voice practically screamed *Why aren't you happy that car is gone?* To be honest, I didn't really miss the car itself. It was a reminder of my parents, but I hadn't thought of it that way for years. Without it, though, I was having to take the bus when I managed to secure a few job interviews.

Job interviews that failed spectacularly. The first person took one look at my cast and the fading bruises on my face and neck, and quickly conjured an excuse for ending the interview early. The second person, a few days later, didn't seem put off by my injuries at all. But she wanted to pay me half what I'd been making at my old job for the same work. I tried to negotiate a better salary, and she almost laughed when I tried.

Sitting on my couch, May was slipping through my fingers without any sign of improvement. I still hadn't heard anything from Jen, and if I didn't find a job soon my already overdue bills were going to sever my ability to be in touch with her. The apartment office was calling me every few days to remind me of my overdue rent and the penalties being accrued on my account. I fell back on my lumpy pillow with a groan, throwing an arm over my eyes.

I hadn't touched my sister's room since that first night when I searched for any clues to find where she'd gone. An optimistic part of me buried way, way down kept insisting she would show up at the door one day and things could go back to the way they used to be. When I woke up in the mornings, my first groggy thought was always whether I'd find Jen in her bed.

When the phone started to ring insistently, I was slow to reach out and pat around the coffee table until I felt it under my hand. I pressed the button to answer it without looking and held it to my ear. "What?"

"Jack, it's me."

I sat up in shock, ignoring the ache from my ribs and shoulder as I stood. "Jen? Thank God! Are you okay, sis? Where are you?"

"I can't talk long." Her voice was hushed, almost like she was trying to speak without being heard by someone else. "I just wanted to make sure you're okay. I heard about what happened at Shine."

"Me? Jen, I'm worried about you! Tell me you're okay. Tell me you'll come back home."

"I'm fine, Jack. Working. Don't worry about me, and stop asking questions. How are you doing?"

I could feel the tears starting to fall down my cheeks. "They hurt me, but I'm still here. I'm healing. Please, just tell me what's going on."

"It's complicated," she said with a heavy sigh. "Things here are... different. But I'm fine, Jack. Stay away from Shine, and stay away from Billy. Promise me."

"I promise," I told her sadly, feeling even more wretched for having given up after the beating.

"Look, I'll try to call you again. Just stay away. Don't...."

The line went dead, but I kept calling Jen's name hoping she was still there. I slumped back down on the couch, holding the phone in my lap. I couldn't stop crying, thinking about my sister being with people like Billy and his goons. Hearing her voice stirred up all my worries, and I felt even more afraid for her now than I had before. I'd never forgive myself for being such a horrible brother, driving her to hang out with the people that pulled her away from me.

NOW

As soon as we were back in the monster truck, I ripped open the packaging of my new phone and started the activation process. Nyk was staring at nothing, his hands hanging from the wheel like he couldn't decide what to do. That scared me more than anything. For all the years I'd known him, I'd never seen the bounty hunter show any fear or hesitation. The man even tangled with a rabid werewolf one time when we were working a case of college kids being murdered on campus.

"How does the Magpie know I'm looking for him," he asked, almost as if speaking to himself.

"I think we're dealing with an organization, not just a person. Who hired you, Nyk? We need to talk to them. Now."

"What?" He shook his head and turned his focus on me. "You know I don't talk about my employers, Jack. Anonymity is part of the service."

"I think they'll be glad if you break it this time. You heard creepy phone guy. They're going after whoever hired you."

Nyk was silent for half a minute, and I could see he was struggling against one of his long-time tenets. Finally, he nodded and pulled out a phone that looked like a toddler's toy in his giant hand. His fingers tapped at the screen with surprising delicateness, and then I could hear the phone ringing through the truck's speakers.

The fifth ring was cut off as the call was answered. "Mr. Walsh. Have you found the Magpie already?" The voice belonged to a man, and it sounded highly educated and cultured. There was a nasal tone that made me think of upper east coast accents.

"Sir, I haven't found much yet, but we were contacted by someone who works for the Magpie. He intimated that you might be in danger, and I felt it was in both our interests for me to warn you. I don't know what we're dealing with it, but it's definitely bigger than just one person."

There was a chuckle over the line. "I assure you that I'm quite safe, Mr. Walsh. Even the Magpie's people can't touch me where I am." I heard a faint rustling sound in the background, like papers being shuffled. "If you're feeling less confident about your ability to track the Magpie..." The sentence was left hanging, and I could see Nyk's mouth working at the implication. That more than anything cleared his prior hesitation.

"No, sir. I agreed to do the job, and it will get done. We've tracked down some businesses that appear to have been owned by companies the Magpie controlled until they were sold six or seven years ago. I'll call you once I have something more concrete."

"You keep using 'we', Mr. Walsh. Who is it that's working with you?"

"Jack Dahlish," I said. "I'm an investigator with a special area of expertise. Nyk and I work together now and then."

71

"Ah, Mr. Dahlish. I've heard good things about you." I raised my eyebrows and shared a look with Nyk. He only shrugged. "Good luck to both of you. I feel confident you will succeed."

"What the hell?" I asked, after the click of the call disconnecting. "Who is this guy, and how does he know who I am?"

The bounty hunter cracked a grin. "You don't think someone who hired me to find the Magpie knows about you and the Nox?"

"Okay, yeah, that makes sense when I actually think about it. But who is he?"

Nyk shook his head. "Can't tell you, Jack. Frankly, I don't even know. He called me with references I trust, though, so I was willing to put up with the anonymous client." He turned and started the truck, smoothly shifting gears and backing out of the parking space. "I got half up front, too, which was really nice."

"I wish some of my clients would pay like that," I grumbled. "I still have a couple dozen I have to call every few weeks just to get twenty or thirty bucks toward their bills." The prepaid phone was finally active, and I stared at the screen full of useless preloaded apps. I wasn't sure what to do next, since we'd used up the one lead I'd managed to scrape up. Nyk surprised me by turning confidently out of the lot. "Where are we going?" I asked.

"I have a few ideas for people who might have been visited by the Magpie's agents the last few years. We're going to check in with them and see what they have to say."

That was an area I hadn't considered, but then I wasn't in a position to know much about who might have dealt with the Magpie in the past. Obviously, since I was the moron who thought he'd taken the Magpie out of the picture years ago.

Thanks to the talisman I wore, I was one of nine humans in the world that had the ability to sense the supernatural beings. That put me in a position of being a kind of policeman for the supernatural world, tracking down and putting a stop to anyone breaking the rules against harming humans. I even got called in when groups of Nox had differences they couldn't work out between themselves.

As a result of all that, there weren't many Nox who looked at me in a friendly light. There were those like Chip who I knew and spoke with, but there was always a guardedness when they were around me. It's the same way that regular people feel when they're driving along and notice a cop car nearby. You know you're not doing anything wrong, after you drop your speed a bit, but you can't help but be aware of the officer in your vicinity and worry that you're going to do something to call attention to yourself.

Nyk drove us out to an upscale neighborhood on the north side of town, between the loops. The houses here were shaded by old growth oak trees, and they had the look that screamed old money. Don't get me wrong, there were a lot of Nox families with the generational wealth to live in a place like this, but I wouldn't have expected to find someone desperate enough to deal with the Magpie. The drive we pulled into was long and circled a large fountain in front of a house set far back from the road. A gate barred our entry, and Nyk turned off the truck so he could be heard as he leaned out to press the button on an intercom.

"Nyk Walsh, here to see Skel."

"Skel?" I asked as he pulled his head back into the vehicle. "What kind of name is that?"

"His real name is Chester, but he's been called Skel for years. Short for skeleton, an old school nickname that stuck."

We waited for several minutes before the intercom finally buzzed and the gate began to pull back. Nyk started the truck and pulled slowly along the drive to park on the far side of the fountain. As I slid down to the ground a few miles below the bottom of the door, I looked around at the immaculately groomed yard. There were hedges in the shape of animals, honest to God. I never thought I'd see that outside of TV shows or movies, but there it was. It felt like showing off how much money you had, enough to pay someone to waste hours doing something so pointless.

The door of the house opened, and a little kid came running down the flagged path. "Nyk," he called out in a piping voice. "Too long, old man."

"Hey, Skel." The bounty hunter held out a massive fist for the kid to bump, and I had to do a double take. He wasn't a kid after all, just a very small man with an emaciated frame. I shuddered at memories of pictures I'd seen of refugees and concentration camp survivors.

Skel turned to look at me curiously, and then I saw recognition bloom in his eyes. "Yo, what's up with bringing the po po?"

"My reputation proceeds me once again," I said, trying to smile reassuringly. My fingers were touching the amulet through my coat and shirt as I opened myself to view the Nox essence. It's almost impossible to describe how it felt every time I did that, but the closest approximation is when you feel like you're about to throw up and you're begging your body not to vomit. Except that the feeling lasts for the entire time I keep myself open to the supernatural world.

The first thing I felt was warmth, a feeling that made me think of a nice fire in the hearth while I enjoyed a cup of tea on a quiet evening. The air around the little creature was filled with a silver haze, almost sparkling in the sunlight. His appearance shifted in my new vision, seeing through his human mask to the misshapen and wrinkled true visage. Combined, it all told me exactly what kind of Nox I was facing, a common household creature often called a brownie.

"You and me, old man. Inside. He stays here!" The emaciated childlike creature pointed at me with a glare before turning and retreating into the house. I shrugged and watched Nyk walk down the path. The door closed behind him, and I was left alone to continue admiring the house and grounds.

Almost an hour later, the door opened again. Nyk stood in the doorway talking to someone I couldn't see for a bit, laughing loudly at something they said. He was wiping tears of mirth from his eyes as he approached the truck.

"Well? Get anything from him?"

"Yep," he said, keeping quiet until we were back in the truck and moving again, turning out of the house's driveway. "Skel's family went through some rough times four years ago. His mom got offended by something one of their patrons did or said, as brownies are wont to do, and they lost a lot of income for a while. He was out one day, and these two people come up to him. Dressed in the whole secret spy getup; black suit, white shirt, black tie, sunglasses."

Well, that was starting to sound familiar.

"They said they worked for someone who was willing to pay good money for things that wouldn't be missed too much. Valuable things, but only to the right buyer. Well, these two must have done some homework, because they offered a price that was exactly the amount that Skel's family was missing out on from the patron. It had been a few months at this point, so it was hard to resist."

"I can imagine. What did they want him to 'acquire' and sell them?"

"He doesn't remember."

"Huh?" I turned to look at Nyk in confusion.

"Skel says there are three days missing. He remembers the suits and their offer, remembers considering it, and then the next thing he has a memory of is sitting on his couch looking at a duffel bag full of cash."

I tried to process that information, hating how difficult it was going to make our investigation. It's pretty hard to find someone you know is buying rare and sometimes stolen objects,

76

if you can't find out exactly what they bought. "Nothing missing from his house, or from his family's patrons?"

Nyk shook his head. "Not a thing."

"What about the cash? Anything odd there that could point us in a direction?"

"Deposited in small chunks over several months to avoid governmental eyes. Skel said it was all in fives and tens, which he found a little odd."

"Not that odd, really, if the Magpie has his fingers in some illegal businesses and is using that cash to pay for these purchases. It doesn't give us much to go on, though. I hope your next candidate is more helpful."

He'd been driving south during our conversation, and it wasn't long before we were pulling to the curb a few blocks from my office. I was afraid he might be kicking me out to check more leads on his own, but Nyk slid out of the truck as soon as it came to a stop and waited for me on the sidewalk. Once I joined him, he waved for me to follow. It didn't take long before I felt a sinking feeling that I knew where we were going.

A lot of homeless people set up little tent camps under the interstate overpasses half a mile from the building where my office was. It was also the place you had to go to visit one of my least favorite Nox, a strigoi named Selma. She could answer the unanswerable, but in return you had to relive some of your worst memories and put up with riddles for answers that would drive you crazy before you ever figured out their meaning.

I sighed with happy relief when Nyk turned aside before we reached Selma's overpass. Instead, we approached Milam Park. It was sunny and fairly warm for January, but still cold enough that few people were lingering to enjoy an afternoon in the park. The playground was deserted, and the gazebo was hosting one young couple who were very close to each other. As we approached a bench in a shady corner of the park, I could make out a bundle of old clothes. The smell hit me a few steps later, the odor of unwashed body and cheap booze. I guess Chip didn't take my advice and head to the YMCA, after all.

One muddy brown eye opened, took several seconds to focus, and then latched on to me. "Dahlish," the old goblin chortled. "I was on my way to take a shower, when this angel appeared and pointed out a two for one special." He held up a bottle of gin that looked hilariously oversized in his small hand.

"What the hell?" I asked Nyk. "There's no way Chip ever had anything the Magpie might want to buy."

"You never knew him before this," the bounty hunter said, waving his hand at the huddled figure on the park bench. Then he spoke louder. "Tell Jack how you spent the eighties and nineties, goblin."

"I was a king!" Chip cried out in his high-pitched voice. "I owned a hot nightclub, two office buildings downtown, and I drove a red sportscar that made panties melt like butter."

As he started cackling, I could only shake my head. This had to be a joke. Chip had been a mainstay of the streets for as long as I'd been in business, and even when I first met him there had been a sense of permanence about his rough living. How

78

could anyone who ended up this way have ever been so successful.

"And then that little bitch slid into my life," he continued, his voice turning bitter as the laughter died. "She was an absolute bombshell, boys, the kind of woman you'd sell your left foot to spend one night with. I thought she was just another bimbo chasing expensive dinners and gifts of jewelry. I was so wrong."

The pile of clothes started to shake, and for a second I thought he might be laughing again. Then I heard the sounds, and knew he was sobbing over the memories of his lost life. "I never even knew her name, but my one night with her was the best memory I'll ever have. That next morning is the absolute worst.

"I woke up to pounding on my door, and these goons slapped me around for five or ten minutes before throwing me out of my own place. Those bastards even laughed at me, making me stand in the street naked while they stole my car. I was so pissed." I was still trying to deal with the fact that this sounded like the truth, wrapping my head around the homeless drunk having been a wealthy businessman back when I was running around in diapers and on playgrounds.

"Then this big truck arrives, and these burly guys hop out to start taking all my stuff! I miss my paintings the most, after I spent so many years building my collection. I yelled at them, I hit them, I screamed for my neighbors to call the cops on the thieves. But everyone just stood on their sidewalks, staring at me like I was a piece of filth.

"When the cops did finally arrive, they put *me* in handcuffs. I was arrested for trespassing on my own property!" The little goblin shook his head, and I could see his eyes had glazed over as he relived the memories. "I spent two nights in the filthiest cell you can imagine, and they didn't give me any clothes until a pile of smelly rags was pushed through the bars and I was ordered to dress. Once I did, here comes the bombshell walking through the rows of cells. That bitch. And you know what? Not one of those rough and tough prisoners catcalled or offered to slip her some meat.

"She stopped in front of my cell, and just stared at me. A minute, an hour. I don't know how long, but I felt so miserable and angry that I couldn't even think of a word to say. Then she pulls a folded piece of paper from her purse, drops it through the bars, and walks away. Last time I ever saw her. Last time I ever want to see her."

Nyk was watching me through the story, and from the way he was judging my reaction I could tell this was something he'd heard before. My first reaction, after realizing this had actually happened, was embarrassment at the way I'd always looked down on Chip and treated him like an annoyance. I felt bad for the Nox, having to go through something so demeaning.

At the same time, my curiosity was pegging the meter as high as it would go. "What was on the piece of paper, Chip?"

The goblin didn't answer, his form still shaking as he cried out the emotions from the memories. Half a minute later, a small hand poked out of the clothes. A grimy piece of paper was held out, shiny from years of being held and rubbed against his body. I hesitated for a second, but I knew I had to see what was on it. I snatched it from his hand, and gingerly unfolded the page to reveal a copied document composed in elaborately beautiful calligraphy.

I, Cunforth Higgins Inglethorp Prexis, hereby accept the terms laid out and agree to sell all my belongings to the person known as Magpie. In accordance with Covenant rule 37, paragraph 9, subsection III, this agreement can never be reversed.

At the bottom of the page were two signatures. One belonged to Chip, who I now knew to be Cunforth, and the other was the Magpie. That second signature was so blocky and purposeful that it was impossible to tell anything about the person who put it there. It could have almost been printed out from the way it so resembled one of the most common fonts on computer programs.

"Well, shit," I said, folding the paper up again and giving it back to the little Goblin. Mention of the Covenants, a sort of treaty signed more than two hundred years earlier to end open hostility between humans and Nox, gave me the chills. Why would the Magpie go to such lengths to keep things seemingly legal, when he was buying and selling stolen goods? Was the veneer of legitimacy enough to keep people like me from doing anything to stop him? Of course, he was still at work, and the only person who apparently even tried to stop him was myself ten years earlier. So I guess that answered my question.

"I don't understand." I rubbed my forehead, where I could feel a headache starting to throb. "If you sold everything, what happened to the money they gave you?"

The goblin poked his head out of the smelly clothes again, and I could see the greenish tinge on his skin as his disguise slipped in the midst of so much emotion. "I can't remember," he said in a strangled whisper. "I don't even remember agreeing to this, but I got so drunk that night I probably would have signed anything someone put in front of me."

"That has to make it an illegal contract," I said, struggling to remember the terms laid out in the thirty seventh rule of the Covenant. Okay, so I admit that I flipped through my copy only once. It was a few weeks after I'd decided to keep the talisman and accept the responsibility, and this heavy package showed up at my office door. The leather-bound book inside was easily over a thousand pages, written in a script that might have been popular a couple hundred years ago but was exceedingly difficult to read these days.

"By human law," Nyk said. "By the rules of the Covenant, the signature itself is all that's required to make it a binding document. The Nox leaders of the day felt that anyone gullible enough not to know exactly what they were signing deserved whatever happened. Frankly, I don't know if the attitudes of the community have changed that much."

I thought about some of the matriarchs and patriarchs of Nox families, and I couldn't help but agree. No matter how conservative and old-fashioned your human neighbors might be, the Nox could teach them a thing or two about holding on to ideas that were centuries out of date. If not for their willing adoption of new technologies, they could make the Amish look progressive.

"Okay," I said, trying to push my racing thoughts into some kind of order. "This woman who seduced Chip had to be working for the Magpie. Probably a high-level employee, if he trusted her with such a high value operation. We need to find out who she was."

Chip started cackling again, and his bright eyes were staring at me wildly. "Do you think I never tried to find her, Dahlish? I spent years doing nothing else. I would watch my old house, or my club where I'd first seen her, waiting for anything that could lead me back to her. I followed anyone who showed up at either place more than a few times, and it never got me anywhere."

"Well, maybe not back then, but things have changed. What was the name of your club? I can track the ownership records and see where that leads us."

He stared at me for a few moments, then his eyes darted to Nyk. "My club was called Shine."

THEN

In the weeks after the call from Jen, I tried to force myself back to Shine to continue searching for her. Every single time, I would get a few minutes down the road before having to jump off the bus at the next stop because my body was shaking so badly. I kept replaying the beating in the alley in my mind, and I'd feel lightheaded until I gave up and turned back for home.

At the end of May, I finally got a job. It was in a call center for a national retailer. I spent my evenings getting yelled at by people who couldn't wrap their heads around how interest payments worked, or by people who woke up and realized they didn't really need the item they'd bought a day or week before and had already been using. It depressed me how many people thought the company should take back a piece of clothing that had been worn a few times already, or a lawnmower they'd used a few times and decided didn't cut the grass exactly the right way.

Unfortunately, my debts had grown too much during my unemployment. I lost the apartment the week before I got the job and was sleeping on Eddie's couch. He'd been happy to have me for the first few days, but after a couple of weeks I could see he was already trying to work up the nerve to tell me to find someplace else. On top of that, my car still hadn't been found and the cops practically admitted it never would be. I continued riding the bus everywhere I needed to go.

During the second week of June, Eddie finally told me I had to stop staying with him. He'd been dating a woman for a couple of months, and it was starting to get serious. Hard to keep up the romance when you could never take her back to your place without a depressed third wheel dragging everything down. I didn't blame him at all. I could only thank him for giving me a place to stay for so long.

I called other friends, and I kept getting excuses about how it wasn't a good time right now. Maybe next month. I thought about a cheap motel, but my credit card was almost maxed out, and it was already hard enough to meet the minimum payments on it. I was able to get overnight shifts at work, so I would ride the bus during the day and sleep during long routes until I had to get off and hop on the next one. The drivers started to recognize me, though, and while only one gave me grief I felt too humiliated to continue using them.

That's how I ended up in a room at a shelter in late June. Because of my odd work hours, it had been easier to get a bed. I'd catch several hours of sleep in the middle of the day, before the normal crowd started to show up. It was nice to be able to take a shower again, even if it wasn't the cleanest or most pleasant place to do it. I was as low as I'd ever been, but I kept myself going with the thought that in a month or two I'd pay off some of my debt and be able to afford a cheap apartment again.

Through it all, I kept my cell phone paid up. I was hoping Jennifer would call again, to let me know where she was. Even better, a call that she was at our old apartment and wanted to know why she couldn't get in. I was more than willing to admit my failings if it meant she was coming back. I'd even given Mrs. Wisson a sealed letter for Jen, in case she knocked on the old woman's door trying to find me.

When the phone rang one morning, waking me half an hour after I'd fallen asleep, I grabbed for it desperately. "Jen?" I asked, after answering the call. I couldn't remember the last time I'd answered any other way.

But the voice on the other end wasn't my sister. It was the deep tones of a man, with a slight Southern accent on his words. "Is this Mr. Jack Dahlish?"

"Yeah, I'm Jack." Rubbing the interrupted sleep from my eyes, I swung my legs off the creaking cot and walked away from the few other slumbering forms. "Who is this?"

"Mr. Dahlish, my name is Oliver Williams. I'm with the San Antonio police department. Can you tell me the last time you saw your sister? Uhh... a Ms. Jennifer Dahlish."

I felt the blood drain from my face. My mind immediately jumped to a worst-case scenario. "Where is she? What happened to Jen?"

"Please, sir, if you could just answer the question."

"It's been a couple of months," I admitted. "Tell me what happened."

After a short hesitation, I could hear muffled talking. I knew the officer had placed his hand over the phone and was telling someone nearby what I'd said. It didn't take long for his voice to come through clearly again. "Mr. Dahlish, I am going to give you an address. Can you drive out and meet with me, sir?"

"I don't have a car, but I'll take the bus." I deflated as I spoke, knowing that his refusal to tell me anything over the phone had to be a bad sign. I memorized the address he gave me, along with the directions of how to find it from the nearest bus stop. The officer even walked to that stop and gave me the route number, which I appreciated.

It took most of an hour to gather my things and reach the location. I had to transfer buses a few times to get to the right place. The entire time, my body was tense as I willed the drivers to go faster. I was almost rocking in my seat with my impatience. The other passengers around me probably thought I was crazy or stoned out of my mind, but I didn't have the mental space to notice them.

As soon as I bounded off the bus at the stop, I looked wildly around. This was a residential street, with older but nice looking homes lining both sides of it. The only clue for where I needed to go was a police car parked at an angle inside of a cul-de-sac. I hurried over, almost running with my bag of clothes and belongings thumping a steady rhythm against my back with the movement.

The cop car was blocking off a graveled path that led into a wide space between two houses. The officer leaning against the hood straightened and held up a hand as I approached. He was fifteen or twenty years older than me, black, with the stance and physique that said he was ready for any violence that might come his way. His black hair was cut very short, and a tight mustache covered the lip over his mouth.

"Jack Dahlish?" he asked, and I recognized the voice as the one that had spoken to me on the phone.

"Yeah, that's me. Where's my sister?" I turned my attention away from him, looking down the gravel drive and seeing a couple more vehicles farther down. One was an unmarked car, and the other an SUV that had "Crime Lab" written on the side facing me. My heart started to pound faster at the sight, and I had to use all my willpower to keep from dropping to my knees.

"Sir, we don't know if this is your sister or not. There is a body of a young woman back there, and she had a driver's license in her purse with the name of Jennifer Dahlish. That could have been stolen or picked up from somewhere, though."

The words were slow to make it through the buzzing in my ears. When they did, I could only look at the cop with confusion. "Doesn't she look like her picture?"

He grimaced, and the expression told me that even my worst fears weren't enough to cover what was happening. "There's, uh, an issue with making physical identification. I'm sorry to do this, but could you tell me if there are any marks that we could use to identify your sister? Birth marks, or tattoos you might know about?"

I shook my head, still trying to wrap my mind around what was happening. "No tattoos. She had a birth mark as a kid, but it faded away years ago." I tried to think of my sister, shocked to realize that her face was almost fuzzy in my memory. "She had purple hair the last time I saw her."

Officer Williams grunted, looking down the path. "A lot of women these days color their hair, so I don't think we can base anything off that."

"But *she* has purple hair, doesn't she?" I asked, pointing toward the cars a hundred feet away. Swallowing, the cop nodded reluctantly. "I want to see her," I demanded. "I have to know if that's my sister."

"That's really not a good idea, sir." His eyes were pained as they turned back to mine. "She was beat pretty extensively."

My knees went weak, and memories of my own beating flashed back. It had been weeks since the cast came off and the last of my bruises faded, but I'd carry the scars of that night in my head for years to come. Had Jennifer suffered the same thing? Did Billy's thugs beat her until she couldn't take any more, and then dump her here?

Suddenly, I realized Officer Williams was calling my name. His voice was fainter than it should have been, and that's when I realized I was running down the gravel path. My breath was in my ears as I passed the unmarked car and crime scene truck, seeing a placid pond circled by a jogging path. On the far side of the pond from this small parking area, half a dozen people were gathered in two groups. Two detectives were standing on a small wooden bridge that passed over a drainage ditch, leaning against the railing as they watched three crime scene techs combing the overgrown ground for any forensic clues. Another uniformed cop was walking the scene with them, and he looked up at the sound of my running footsteps.

"Hey! You can't be here!"

The detectives turned their heads, and I adjusted my course for whatever was in the overgrown grass. They started to move to intercept, but they'd reacted too slowly as I barreled off the path. My arms were pumping now, my feet slapping the ground and I was in a full sprint. I *had* to find out if that was my sister.

A few steps off the jogging path, my left foot found a gopher hole. I felt sharp pain in my ankle as I tripped and fell face first against the hard ground that hadn't seen rain in a few weeks. I could taste copper in my mouth, where I'd bitten my tongue when my chin impacted the dirt. So much for being healed and not hurting every time I moved.

The irate officer came striding through the tall grass, and roughly grabbed my right arm to jerk me onto my feet. I cried out as I felt a sharp pain in my mostly healed shoulder, and he released me as if he'd burned his hand. His face was still closed down in frowning disapproval, though. "This is a crime scene, fella. Turn around and march out of here before I arrest you and toss you in a cell."

"It's okay, Roger," a voice puffed behind me. I turned my head just enough to see Officer Williams jogging up. "This is the guy I called. Possible brother."

"Well, I'm sorry for your loss, but you can't come charging into a crime scene. Do you want whatever animal killed this girl to get away with it because you taint the evidence?"

I could feel blood trickling from my mouth, and I raised a hand to wipe it away. "I just need to know if it's her or not. Please, I have to know."

Officer Williams took my shoulder and gently turned me away, escorting me back to the path around the pond. "Mr. Dahlish, I understand how you feel. You have to let us do our job, sir. I promise that as soon as the scene is cleared, I'll do what I can to help you get some answers."

I could only nod, keeping my eyes focused on the pond. As much as I wanted to look and find out if it was Jen, I was afraid to know for sure. Part of my brain kept telling me that if I never looked, she never had to really be dead. It was a messed-up Schrodinger's Cat situation, and only made sense to my grief-stricken brain.

I don't know how long I stood there, entranced by the ripples on the water with every light breeze. I remember seeing faces staring out of windows in the surrounding houses, and a few times groups of people gathered at the entrance of the gravel drive where the two police officers would keep them back. The smell of food intruded once, but the thought of eating just made me nauseous. Not that it mattered, since no one offered me anything.

The late afternoon sun was glinting off the water when Officer Williams approached again. "Mr. Dahlish, they're removing the body. Are you sure you really want to look, sir? I'm telling you, it's bad."

My voice was hoarse when I told him yes, and I could see he was debating with himself on the wisdom of letting me. One of the detectives walked over before he could make a decision. "Ollie, let the guy take a peek. It'll help us to know who this is without waiting for all the DNA and crap. Could help him to not have to wonder, too."

I didn't wait for a response, walking forward as I saw a couple of coroner's attendants carrying a stretcher from the tall grass. That was the first time I noticed the van from the morgue, parked alongside the unmarked car and crime scene SUV. Once they got to the flatter ground of the jogging path, the attendants dropped the wheels of the stretcher. While they were occupied, I reached forward and lifted the sheet.

In the few seconds I was able to look before releasing the sheet with a cry of horror, I saw dried blood and exposed teeth. The nose was a pulpy mess, and the eyes so swollen you could barely make out the lids. Above it all was purple hair, brighter in color than I was used to seeing, above half an inch of brunette roots. That and the familiar V-shaped widow's peak made me almost certain I was looking at what was left of my sister.

Hands grabbed my biceps, pulling me away as I screamed with horror and pain. I must have blacked out, because the next thing I knew I was sitting in the back seat of a police cruiser with a silvered blanket wrapped around me. Officer Williams was crouching beside the open door, concern in his eyes. "Mr. Dahlish?"

"It was her," I said shakenly. "That's my sister." I told him about the hairline, and the color of the roots.

"Sir, there could be hundreds of women in this city with that kind of hair. Thousands."

"Do they all carry a driver's license with my sister's name and face on it?"

I could see that he wanted to reassure me, tell me again that it could have been picked up from somewhere my sister left it. But he also saw how certain I was, and he wouldn't cheapen my feelings. "It's going to take a few days for the lab to verify identity. Her dental records aren't going to help much." He winced and turned away, realizing how bad that must sound. I'd seen the shape of her mouth, the shattered remains of teeth that must have taken serious punishment. "Would you be willing to provide a DNA sample, so we have something for comparison?"

When I consented, he stepped away to grab one of the crime scene techs, and they ran a swab over the inside of my cheek. My tongue had stopped bleeding, and the scrape on my chin throbbed more than hurt, but a paramedic had been called in to look me over. Once she pronounced me capable of caring for myself, I was escorted to the bus stop.

"Take this," Officer Williams said, holding out a card with his name on it. "A detective will call you when they get the results from the DNA tests, but if you have any questions, feel free to call me." He looked at me until I nodded and slid the card into a pocket. "I really hope it turns out to not be your sister, Mr. Dahlish. But if it is, do you have any idea where we could start looking for whoever did this?"

I opened my mouth, meaning to tell him everything. About my sister running away, tracking down Billy, my visit to Shine, the beating in the alley. Instead, "I don't know, officer. It's been almost two months since I saw her, and we only spoke once on the phone since then."

93

The cop could tell I was holding something back, but then he was probably used to that. Shock, the need to keep a family secret that seems more important than it really is, or even willful ignorance of things a person had seen with their own eyes and chosen to ignore. The police probably saw it all every week. "If you do think of something, no matter how small, call me. Or just call the main SAPD number and ask for Detective Margolis. He's the lead on the case."

The sun was already sinking below the houses when my bus finally pulled up to the stop. I trudged up the few stairs and fell into a seat, feeling worn out and exhausted. My sister was dead, and I'd done nothing to help her. How could I live with that?

NOW

Nyk parked his behemoth of a truck two blocks away from the entrance of the club, and we sat in silence for several minutes looking at the dilapidated building. The entire area was old warehouses and storage buildings that had been around for decades, most with seemingly little to no upkeep. That feeling of being in a bad neighborhood had been a large part of the attraction that drew people to a club here. But now it looked deserted and vacant, and there were no signs near the door to tell you it had ever existed.

"Did you know?" I asked, not taking my eyes from the building.

"Not the name of the club, but I knew Chip's story. It was the big rumor when I got to town in '08, people still talking about it years after it happened. Never openly, and definitely not with any names, but they talked about it all the same. A few even pointed out the little homeless guy a time or two and would say something like 'If you ever think of messing with the wrong people, just look at him.' It was the kind of thing you often hear in a new city, though."

"The fucking Magpie," I said through gritted teeth. "There's no way Billy Wish was old enough to have been operating in the early nineties. He barely looked old enough to be doing business in 2010. So who the hell was Chip dealing with?"

"Slow down, Jack. You don't even know if Billy was human or Nox. There are plenty of them that can live for centuries."

I could only shake my head. "No, he went down too easy to be a Nox."

Nyk clearly wanted to argue that point, but he sighed and gave it up. "If Chip was dealing with someone else, then we're left with two options. Either you took down someone who wasn't really the Magpie, or that title passes to different people whenever necessary."

"The Dread Pirate Roberts of the Nox world?" I asked around a snort. But the more I thought about it, the more sense it made. I didn't like to admit I could have been wrong, too, so the thought that the title just passed to someone else was somewhat comforting. "If that's the case, it's going to be really hard to track down whoever is claiming the title now."

"That's why we keep doing what we've been doing. Follow the financials. We know this club was functioning and profitable as late as 2015, and then it was sold to a club promoter from Houston looking to expand his reach. Attendance and profit went quickly downhill from there."

"Yeah, because the club catered to Nox. The humans who made their way here only came back because they could feel it was a dangerous place, which excited them. Once the Nox stopped coming, it lost the appeal."

"Owned by yet another shell company, Urocissa Ornata, named after another species of bird in the magpie family. Are

you sure those fancy websites won't let you connect dots between the four shell companies we know about?"

I had spent half an hour searching the company names
fruitlessly on my phone while we sat in front of the shuttered
club. I was able to track company addresses, all outside of the
United States and usually in countries with lax banking laws.
Beyond that I'd found very little. I needed more time with my
laptop, where I could go at the search harder. "Get me back to
my office, and I'll keep trying. Do you think you can track
down Ordoñez tonight?" That was the name of the man who'd
taken over as club manager after Billy Wish.

"Shouldn't be that hard. We know he still lives in town, so
I just need to check around with the other clubs to find out if
he's working there. Maybe he made a lateral move into the
hospitality industry, so I'll check out hotels and restaurants."

Once back in front of my building, Nyk stopped in the road
long enough for me to slide out of the truck and give him a tired
wave. A little compact car behind him had the temerity to honk,
and I had to wonder what the driver thought they could do if the
truck didn't move. Were I behind the wheel, I would have lin-
gered longer than usual. Nyk has always been nicer and more
patient, however, so he accelerated smoothly away as soon as I
was clear.

The lack of sleep from the previous night was starting to
catch up to me, and even the energy from my half-awake nap in
my office chair that morning had long ago worn off. But I was
determined to keep going until I found something that we could
check out the next day. People streamed off the elevator as I

waited in the lobby. One or two nodded, but most just seemed excited to leave the building and head home. I was alone on the ride up to my floor, listening to the irritating bland jazz once again.

As soon as I was ensconced behind the desk, my phone started to ring. I groaned at the thought of having to deal with a telemarketer or someone calling to see if I'd do some work for them. The name on the display wiped away any frustration, though, and even sent a spike of adrenaline through my system to wake me up.

"How can I help San Antonio's number one reporter this evening?"

"Jack, you've been neglecting me." The voice on the other end sent shivers up my spine, as always. Karen Kilgraff was a reporter with KRSA, one of the highest rated local channels. She regularly anchored the nightly news, and also did a fair share of field reporting. We'd met a month earlier during the case of the missing children, and somehow the ultra-hot redhead kept in contact with me once that story was over.

"I promise it hasn't been on purpose, Karen. Something dropped into my lap last night, and I've been working all day. It's complicated, but it's an important case for personal reasons."

"Have you eaten?" She asked it sternly, knowing me much better than I ever expected she might.

"I had a burger," I said defensively. My stomach rumbled loudly as if reminding me it hadn't been enough for the entire day.

Karen chuckled, hearing the noise over the phone. "Are you at home or the office?"

"Office," I mumbled, looking through the window at the deepening twilight.

"Stay right there, mister. I've got a few hours before I have to get pretty for the ten o'clock broadcast, so I'm bringing you dinner." She hung up before I could protest or tell her that she was always beautiful enough to be on TV.

While I waited, I opened my laptop and started running searches on the shell companies. Whoever had set them up more than earned what I was sure had to be an exorbitant fee. The companies themselves were owned by other companies, which in turn were owned by yet more companies. Trying to trace the trails back to an original source was like trying to trace a stream of water from within a lake it flowed into.

The best I could come up with was the fact that each trail eventually led me to a company incorporated in Tonga, an island nation in the South Pacific. It seemed awfully coincidental for that many corporations to be based in a string of islands that contained less than a tenth of the population of San Antonio.

I was reading Wikipedia articles about Tonga when my door opened. I looked up and gasped at the beauty of the tall redheaded woman in the door. Karen had a love of the color red that led to always wearing various shades of it. Tonight, she was in a deep vermillion blouse tucked into a dark pink skirt. Her heels matched her blouse. The red always looked so stunning against her creamy skin. Shoulder-length red hair framed a face that was gorgeous enough to have been chiseled from the purest marble.

"Heya, handsome," she said, carrying a bag over to my desk. She leaned over to give me a peck on the cheek, then pulled one of my client chairs around the desk so she could sit near me as she pulled two food containers from the bag. In spite of the flirtatious words and show of affection, Karen and I had never been anything more than friends in the short time we'd known each other. Not that I hadn't been hoping it would turn into more.

"You are an angel," I told her, inhaling the aroma of hand-made ravioli as I opened the lid of the container. Mushroom and spinach, my favorite. I wasted no time, ripping the plastic utensil pack open so I could shovel a bite into my mouth.

"So, tell me about this confounding case you're working on. What's the personal connection?"

I was normally reticent to talk about my sister, even with people I'd known for a few years. Something about Karen made her easy to open up to, though, and before I realized it I was telling her the story of my sister's murder and how Nyk and I were now trying to track down the Magpie. A person I thought I'd taken care of a decade before.

Karen placed a hand on my arm, looking at me with sad eyes. "Jack, I am so sorry about your sister. I wish I could've had a chance to get to know her. I'm sure we would have gossiped about you mercilessly."

"I wish you could have met her, too," I said, realizing just how much I meant it as the words came out. As much as I thought about my sister, I'd never considered how she might have fit into the life I'd made after her passing.

"As for the case, that's a doozy," she said, leaning back in her chair to examine me as I finished the last bites of my ravioli and garlic bread. "Those businesses sound like a good angle, but why were they being sold off in 2014 and 2015 if the person you took down wasn't the real Magpie?"

"Most likely the businesses were a liability, especially since I took up the talisman at the same time I was dealing with the Magpie." I shrugged, realizing I hadn't considered this aspect of the situation as much as I should have. "Nyk and I also have a theory that Magpie is a title that transfers to new people now and then. So maybe with Billy out of the way, someone else took over and decided to take things in a different direction."

Karen smiled, reaching out to rub a bit of sauce from my lip. "Jack, if the businesses were a liability, they wouldn't have waited years before selling. Your other idea is a good one, but I'd still like to find out why they were sold. Send me the data you have on the holding companies. I have a few sources I trust to look into things like this. They create and obfuscate shell companies all the time as part of the service they provide clients. I'll ask them to take a look as a favor to me."

"If they can track the companies back farther than I did, you'll have my eternal gratitude."

"I don't already?" she asked, raising a pencil thin eyebrow.

"Well, you do, but there's always room for more, right?"

She tapped a fingernail against her teeth. "Yes, I believe I do have room for that." Karen leaned forward quickly, brushing her lips against mine before standing to carry the chair back to the far side of my desk. "I have to get back to the station. Bianca gets peeved if I don't let her work on my makeup and hair for at least fifteen minutes before we go live. Call me tomorrow, and we can trade updates."

I was still sitting stunned in my chair as she breezed through the door, surprised by the whisper of a kiss. I knew it probably meant nothing. Was almost positive it meant nothing. But my brain was running wild and celebrating as if I'd just won the Super Bowl.

Finally, I shook it off and forced myself to turn back to work. There would be time later to lie awake wondering if it meant something or nothing. For now, I had to keep following the Magpie down the rabbit hole he had disappeared into after 2010. My next lead was the little brownie, Skel. The Magpie bought something from him, and somehow wiped his memory of it. Was that to cover the tracks of illegal activity? Chip had no memory of signing away his life, as well, so there was something there.

There had to be a connection on the memory angle. Perhaps some kind of drug the person was forced to take after signing the contract. Or perhaps some form of Nox with abilities to wipe memories. A couple of possibilities came to mind, and I pushed my chair over to my file cabinets to unlock the drawers. For years, I had gone to the public library to do research on the books there, but I finally decided to order copies of my own so I could pull them out at any time.

My first selection was a thick volume on Japanese myths. Flipping through, I found a couple of creatures with abilities that could allow them to steal or suppress memories. The first was the baku, a creature described as having the ability to eat nightmares. Often depicted in the form of a tiger with the head and trunk of an elephant, the baku were also considered to be protectors against evil. I know each person's view of what constitutes good and evil can be radically different, but I couldn't see such a Nox participating in wiping memories purely for profit.

The second thing I found was the satori, a creature known for reading minds and speaking the words a person was thinking before they could. These creatures were often met on mountain paths, sometimes said to eat victims after reading their thoughts. I couldn't see that turning into wiping memories, but it wouldn't be the first time an old folktale described a Nox's abilities incorrectly.

Strigoi had the ability to feed off memories, as my prior visits to Selma had shown me, but I retained those memories after she was done with me. Her kind fed more from the emotions conjured by the memories. Even if she could make them disappear, Selma never left her little shadow world. I couldn't imagine someone agreeing to visit her, especially if they knew what she was.

It was surprising how many creatures I could find with the ability to influence dreams. As I made my way through the books, a page of my notebook was filled with the possibilities. Several were well-known, such as the Nightmare and the Sand-man, but those I could strike from the list. There was only one of each, and I knew that both were outside of North America at the moment.

By the time I closed my reference books and slid them back into my file cabinet, my eyes were burning and the headache that had been building all day was pounding in my head. I thought about tuning in to watch Karen on the news, but when I checked my phone, I found it was hours past the last newscast of the night. I was feeling the effects of only getting a few hours' sleep the night before, and glad to shut off the lights and shuffle down the hall on my way home.

THEN

"I'm sorry to say this, Mr. Dahlish, but the tests show a match. It is your sister."

It took three days to get that call. Three days of torture as I kept telling myself it was Jen, while also trying to convince myself I had been wrong, and my sister was still alive. "Did you find the dirtbag who beat on her, yet?"

"We can't divulge information about an ongoing case, sir. I will tell you that we have a number of leads that we're following. A few of them look very promising." The detective didn't sound that hopeful. In fact, he sounded like he wanted to get me off the phone as quickly as possible.

"Have you brought people in for questioning? At least tell me that."

"I'm sorry, sir, that's not information I can provide. If you'd like to call our victim resource line—"

I stabbed the button to end the call, slamming the phone down on the empty seat beside me. An older lady in the next aisle on the bus glanced over at me, her mouth turned down in a disapproving frown. Whether at me for being so loud on the phone or because of the subject, I neither knew nor cared. I turned to watch the buildings slide by, fuming at the delays. My hand strayed to the back pocket where my wallet was kept. I still had the card the officer on the scene had given me.

Making up my mind, I pulled the card out and punched the number into my phone. I listened to the rings, my fingers tapping nervously on my leg. Just as I was about to hang up, I heard the click of the call being answered. "Officer Oliver Williams speaking. How may I help you?"

"Hello," I said, suddenly nervous. "This is Jack Dahlish. We, uh, met three days ago out by the pond on the north side of town?"

"Yes, sir. How can I help you?"

"I just heard from the detective that the DNA test I submitted came back as a familial match on the body. It was definitely my sister." My voice caught on the last words, and I had to stop and collect myself.

"I'm sorry to hear that, Mr. Dahlish. I know how hard it can be to lose a family member."

"Thank you. I, uh, was wondering if you'd be able to tell me anything about the investigation?"

There was silence for several seconds. "I'm not permitted to divulge details of a current investigation."

"That's the thing," I said, trying to rein in the frustration in my voice. "The detective won't tell me anything, just says there are so-called leads they're following. There is this guy that Jen met at a club called Shine several months ago. One of her friends said they dated a time or two. Billy Wish. You guys should check him out!"

"Have you mentioned this man to the detectives in charge of the case? Why would you suspect his involvement with your sister's death?"

Officer Williams had one of those soothing voices that seemed to lull away any anger, and it was working on me. Or maybe it was because I'd gotten little sleep the last two days, thrashing around in the sheets of my bed at the shelter. "Can I tell you something without it becoming a police matter?"

He paused again, and I had the feeling he was moving away from other people. "Mr. Dahlish, are you going to say anything that could be construed as committing a criminal act?"

"No!" I said, indignant that he would think such a thing.

"Very well, then I'm willing to hear you out. But not over the phone." I could hear a sound in the background, a noise that made me think of when sirens blooped for half a second on TV. "Meet me tomorrow morning, at the coffee shop on Blanco just north of 410. You familiar with the area?"

It was a location only a few miles from my job, an easy bus trip after my overnight shift was completed. "Sure. I can be there by eight?"

"I'll see you then, Mr. Dahlish. Take care."

Setting the phone down much more gently this time, I felt better than I had in days. Maybe the officer would provide me with some information about the case, even if it was just the barest crumb. It would be better than the wild speculation running rampant in my brain at all hours. Even when I was speaking on the phone at work, trying to talk customers through the many issues they couldn't seem to stop creating for themselves, I was thinking of my sister. Seeing that shattered face under blood-soaked purple hair.

When I walked into the small coffee and donut shop, I was tired from a full night of work but feeling elated at the prospect of getting information. It took a lot of willpower to keep from making a cops and donuts joke as I approached Officer Williams, who stood and shook my hand. "Thanks for meeting me," I said.

He was already in uniform, the creases on the sleeves sharp. "I know how frustrating it can be in your position, sir. I wish I could do more for you, but there's not much information in the part of the case file I have access to." He wrapped his hands around a large paper cup that was still steaming. Another was sitting in front of me, and he nodded toward it. "I don't know if you drink coffee, but I got one in case you might need it."

I thanked him, feeling truly grateful for the gesture. I dumped two packets of sugar and one serving of creamer into the cup, stirring it slowly. "I'll be glad of any information, officer. It's better than my brain filling in all the blanks."

"Yes, I can imagine." He sighed and cast his eyes around the few tables to make sure no one was close enough to overhear. We were alone except for one harried man at the counter ordering a couple dozen donuts to go. "The detectives have done door-to-door interviews in the neighborhood around the pond and jogging trail. They couldn't find anyone with knowledge of your sister, or anyone who might have seen her the previous evening. Do you know if any of her friends might have lived in that area?"

I shook my head. "I thought about that. The nearest friend I know of is probably half a mile from that little park. I've never even been in that neighborhood until... well, that day."

"The only other piece of information I could find was an attached report from a patrol woman three weeks back. She gave your sister a warning for solicitation and loitering outside one of those cash for gold stores. I put in a call to the officer to see if she remembers the incident, but haven't heard back yet."

"Solicitation?" I'd heard the term many times on cop shows, and never in a good connotation. "Does that mean she was, uh, taking money for sex?" I couldn't believe my sister would ever resort to such a thing.

He was quick to reassure me. "No, nothing like that. Especially not in the area of the incident. Most likely, she could have been passing out flyers or something like that. Maybe annoying people with one of those 'can you take a quick survey' things. Business owners complain about that sort of activity, afraid it will keep customers from entering their store."

My shoulders slumped in relief. It was good to know my sister hadn't gone that far without turning to me for help. "What about this cash for gold place? Does the owner remember her?"

Officer Williams fidgeted a bit, not meeting my eyes. "I don't know. If the detectives have visited, those notes are behind a barrier my access won't get me past. You have to understand, sir, that most investigations aren't wrapped up in forty-eight hours like you might see on TV. It can take weeks or even months of questioning people and following up on leads."

"If they were doing any of that, I think they'd tell me." A wary look in the older man's eyes told me I'd hit a mark. He was worried that my sister's case was being neglected just as much as I was. "Officer Williams, would you tell me which store my sister was at when she received the warning? I'd like to go down there myself, see what I can find out."

"I really don't think it's a good idea to do that, son. Stepping on the detective's toes won't help anyone in the long run."

"There have to be toes there to step on," I muttered into my coffee, taking a deep sip. "What about Billy Wish? Has anyone looked into him?"

"I ran his name through our databases. Nothing there, not even a driver's license. Either he gave you a fake name, or he's never been entered into the system." He leaned back, and I could see there was something bothering him. I waited as patiently as I could. "That club, though. Shine? There are some strange things going on over there. I asked around, to see if a few of the guys that patrol the area knew anything. They were quick to tell me that club is off limits."

"Off limits?"

"It's not something I'm proud of, but there are places around the city we aren't allowed. Sometimes the owner has major pull with the mayor or city council, sometimes we just get unofficial word from above to stay away. It doesn't mean anything illegal is happening there, but they don't want cops around."

I turned the half empty cup of coffee on the table, debating with myself. I didn't like to hear that the club was given special

110

status, especially after what had happened to me there. "Officer, how long after being physically assaulted can charges be filed?"

"Well, the statute of limitations is two years for physical assault in Texas. It's pretty hard to prove anything if you don't report it at the time of the incident, though. Why are you asking, Mr. Dahlish?"

Trying to keep my voice steady, I told him about the beating I'd suffered in the alley behind the club and the events leading up to it. He grunted when I told him what Billy had said about selling something more powerful than drugs, and again when I described waking up in Austin.

"Smart of them to take you out of the jurisdiction. Even if you tried to press charges, the cops in Austin wouldn't have the ability to arrest people in San Antonio. And the cops here would look at your story with heavy skepticism when you're over an hour away." He rubbed a finger over his mustache, a habit I would come to see as a sign of deep concentration. "I believe you, sir, but I don't know that there's much we can do. The city attorneys wouldn't touch it with a ten-foot pole so many weeks after the fact. You could probably get a civil lawyer and go after them that way. Less burden of proof, but you'd still have to make the jury more certain than not that you were assaulted by the people you claim assaulted you."

The optimism I'd felt before the meeting was draining away. In three full days of investigation, the cops had gotten nowhere. I couldn't even tell if they were really looking, or just relegating my sister to the long list of unsolved murders. There was a growing certainty inside me that Billy Wish was involved in some way, but my only avenue of putting pressure on him seemed unlikely to provide any results for months. If then.

He leaned forward, lowering his voice. "I've been wrestling with this for three days, but I have to say it. There was something... off about that park. It's hard to explain, but every time I got close to where your sister was left, I felt a darkness around me." My nervous rotating of the coffee cup stopped as I went still with the words. I'd felt the same thing, a sensation I couldn't put into words. "Whatever happened there, I don't think it's the kind of thing we're prepared for. If I didn't know better, I'd say there was some sort of evil presence left behind."

Officer Williams stood up, reaching over to toss his empty cup into a nearby trash can. "I'm sorry I couldn't provide more information, Mr. Dahlish. You have my number, so call me if you want to talk about this. I really do know what you're going through, and it's not something you should try to work out on your own."

I finished my coffee in silence, leaving a few minutes later. Shuffling along to the bus stop, I couldn't get Shine and Billy Wish out of my head. The female bodyguard had told me that my sister was "with them", whatever that meant. They had to be involved in some way, or know something that could point me toward another path. As much as I dreaded the thought of going back to the club, it was drawing me in.

On the bus ride to the shelter, I noticed a man a few rows ahead of me with his head turned in my direction. I could feel his eyes burning into me, but when I glanced up, his gaze was

112

directed through the window in front of me. He had a large beaklike nose, with a weak chin that led to a scrawny neck. His brown hair and week-old beard were wild and ungroomed. His eyes, when they drifted in my direction before quickly darting away again, were a bright green.

I was so absorbed in trying to watch the man in my peripheral vision that I almost missed my stop. The bus driver had closed the doors when I recognized the buildings and jumped up. My profuse apologies didn't abate the glares that followed me down the short stairs and out of the bus. I half expected the man to follow, but when I turned and looked through the windows of the departing bus he was still in his seat. His eyes locked on mine this time, and I saw a small smirk on his thin lips.

Shaking my head in confusion, I pushed through heavy glass doors to enter the shelter. The building was owned and operated by a local church, and they offered a bed for one week. Two, if you could show records of employment to prove you were trying to pull yourself out of whatever situation made you homeless. There were two nights left until I reached the end of my stay, and I wasn't sure what I was going to do then. My first paycheck would arrive at the end of the week, a day after I lost my bed, and I needed that to have a chance at securing a cheap apartment.

An old woman sat behind a low desk inside the door, and she smiled up at me as I entered. "There you are, dear," she said. "I expected you an hour ago. Someone dropped off a package for you after you left last night."

I stopped in my tracks, my thoughts already on the cot that had been assigned to me in a room with five others. No one should have even known I was there, since I was too embarrassed to admit I was staying in a shelter. Eddie had even called me a few times to ask where I was staying, feeling bad about kicking me out of his place. I just told him I'd found another couch to crash on, and avoided questions of where.

As I approached the desk, the woman pulled a brown parcel from a cubby hole. It was wrinkled and looked to have been handled a lot, wrapped in layers of brown tape. It was the size of a small hardcover book, perhaps nine inches by six. The package felt light, but a tingle ran through my body as I held it.

I was staggered when I turned the package over and saw the flowing script. My name was the only thing written on the package, in a hand that I would know anywhere. Jen had always had the most beautiful handwriting, such a contrast to my barely legible chicken scratch.

"Where did this come from?" I asked hoarsely.

"A young man dropped it off. He was a nice boy. We chatted about the Spurs for a few minutes before he asked to see you. He left the package when he found out you weren't here."

"What did he look like?" Had it been one of my friends, somehow tracking me down? Why would they have a package for me from my sister?

"Oh, he was..." She stopped, staring into space. "You know, I can't really remember what he looked like. Isn't that strange?"

I wanted to grab her shoulders and shake her until she answered me. How can you spend several minutes chatting with someone and not remember what they look like the next morning? The package drew my attention, though, and before I realized it I was walking away. I followed the familiar path to the room where my cot was, dropping onto it without taking my eyes off the package. When I remembered my backpack was still on my shoulders, I didn't even strip it off and drop it to the floor as I normally would.

The package felt smooth under my hands, as if it had passed through other hands for years and the rough edges had been worn away. I tried to find an edge of tape I could peel back to begin unwrapping, but it was an impossible task. I stared at my sister's handwriting for what could have been minutes or hours, lost in my thoughts. The loud footsteps of someone else entering the room shook me back to reality, and I looked up to see a poorly dressed man in his middle age standing beside another cot. We shared a nod.

Without the ability to peel the tape, I had to find some way to cut open the package. For understandable reasons, knives and scissors were hard to find in the shelter. I finally had to backtrack to the older lady at the entry desk, and she was able to cut a small strip off the top of the package.

"Oh!" she said in surprise, catching a glimpse of the box inside. "This is quite a nice little present." With a genuinely happy smile, she passed the parcel over.

I retreated back to my room before pulling the slim box from the packaging. It was black, and the exterior had a velvety

115

feeling. It spoke of quality and expensiveness, even before I saw the gilt lettering that said it had come from a local jewelry store. There was a small clasp, holding the case closed. With shaking fingers, I unlatched and lifted the lid.

Gold flashed, and I snapped the case closed. I looked around, making sure the other man in the room wasn't being nosy. He was lying on his cot, back turned with his face toward the wall. I twisted around, as well, making sure he couldn't see inside the case if he did suddenly roll over. I'd been staying in the shelter long enough to know that you didn't flash around gold anything.

I lifted the lid slowly and tilted my head to look inside the case. The first thing I saw was the coin, silver but with gold accents forming the male profile in the center and the elaborate writing around the edges. My first thought was to wonder how such a coin could be stamped out. I'd never seen one made from two different metals before, and the edges were so flaw-less I could only imagine it had taken a skilled craftsman hours to produce. There was a small hole in the coin, above the man's profile. A silver chain passed through it, the links almost deli-cate looking. I couldn't find a clasp on the chain, or any other way for it to have been attached after looping through the coin.

The writing on the coin was unfamiliar, entirely unlike any other language I'd ever seen. I tried to make out individual let-ters, but as I concentrated on them I felt an ache behind my eyes. It grew more painful, until I finally dragged my attention away from the letters to look at the face in profile once more. It was a stern face, with a sharp chin and strong jaw. The eyes were deep set, below wavy hair that flowed back from the forehead.

I felt a presence nearby, and snapped the case closed to look around. My roommate was still on his cot, facing the wall. There was no one else in the room, and the doorway was empty. I got up to close the door, and as I did the packaging shifted and the corner of a piece of white paper appeared from within the brown paper. I sat back down and pulled the notecard-sized paper from the parcel. It was bright white, almost painfully bright against the brown tape and packaging it had come from. My sister's writing flowed across it.

Jack, I hope you never read this. If you are, then it means something happened to me and I'm probably not coming back. Take care of this Relic, and don't let it out of your sight. I'm sorry I couldn't be there to explain, but this is important. If I'm dead, this is what I died to protect. I've given this package to one of the few people I know I can trust, and told him to take it to you if he doesn't hear from me every day. Jen

I ran my fingers across the writing. It was in purple ink. Of course. My sister's favorite color, the one that was always most predominant in everything she owned. I looked from the note to the case, wondering what she had gotten involved in, to come into possession of such a thing. Opening the case again, I reached out to touch the coin. As soon as my finger made contact, the hairs on my arm stood up and I felt as if lightning had just passed through me.

A cough from behind made me snap the case closed again, and I slid it back into the packaging along with Jen's note. I looked around for my backpack, finally realizing it was still on my back. The case slid into a pocket on the side with ease, leaving enough room to zip the compartment closed. I pushed the backpack under the cot, and then lay back to stare up at the white ceiling.

Directly above me was a brown water stain, which my brain had convinced me looked like a sheep. I stared at it, thinking about the coin in the case and my sister's note. Why had she capitalized the R in relic? Was she killed because someone was looking for the necklace? It certainly seemed to be an item worth a great deal of money.

Over it all, I kept hearing Billy Wish. *A taste of power that your puny little brain couldn't even begin to grasp.*

NOW

I cracked open an eye, almost expecting to see Nyk standing in the corner of my bedroom again. With a sigh of relief, I found myself alone. A glance at my phone on its stand beside the bed showed that my alarm would be going off in less than half an hour. I'd been so exhausted by the time I fell into my bed the previous evening that I'd slept through the night without any dreams that I could remember. It was a rare occurrence, with my overactive mind.

Groaning, I rolled over and pulled the covers over my head. I really wanted to just fall back to sleep, but now that I'd woken enough for my brain to start working all I could think about was the long list of things that needed to be taken care of. After a few minutes of laziness, I rolled out of bed and dragged myself into the bathroom to take a quick shower and get dressed.

When I walked back into the bedroom, there was a voice mail on my phone. I tapped a few buttons to play it, listening to the rumble of Nyk's voice as he told me he needed to meet with a few informants. They were the kind of people who would be spooked by seeing a stranger, so he would meet me at my office when he was done.

Over the next several hours, I checked out a few Nox hotspots looking for any sign of those with the ability to alter or erase memories. I struck out at every location, ramping up my frustration level. I felt like all I needed was one break to get a handle on the case. If I could find one of the Magpie's agents, I could trace that person back to the head of the organization.

I was a few blocks from parking near my office building when my phone rang with a special ringtone. The Chris de Burgh song was one of those oldies that would get stuck in your head for hours, and the association with the person calling made it very special to me.

"Jack, it is ungodly early. Why am I even awake?"

I looked at the clock on my dash, snorting in amusement. "It's already past eleven, Karen. I don't think you can call that early."

"You know I need my beauty sleep, darling."

"If you get any more sleep, you'll be too beautiful to even look at. My heart already wants to pound out of my chest when I see you."

"You little charmer," she said, a smile in her voice. "I want you to know that I'm up before noon solely because of you. My contact in the finance world sent me a report this morning, and you aren't going to believe what he's found."

"He?" I asked, trying to contain a twinge of jealousy. I knew it was stupid, considering how many sources I'd come to learn that Karen used for her job as a reporter. Something about a high-flying financial genius struck a nerve, though. Maybe because it's what I'd once imagined myself becoming. I could imagine some handsome older gentleman in an expensive suit taking her out for dinners at the best restaurants in town. All the things I couldn't afford.

120

If Karen heard my tone, she ignored it. "Axel is one of the best at what he does. Unfortunately, what he does is hide money in all kinds of creative places so that people can get away with paying no taxes on it. Or to keep spouses from finding it during divorce proceedings. It's a dirty job, but I suppose there will always be someone willing to pay him to do it."

Hearing the slight tinge of disgust in her voice made me feel infinitely happier. "Did he track down the main owner of all the shell companies?"

"He's not quite that good, Jack. In fact, he said that whoever was hiding the assets for our mysterious Magpie is one of the best he's ever seen."

"You didn't tell him we were looking for the Magpie, did you?" I asked, feeling a stir of panic.

"I only said that a handsome private investigator I know was trying to find someone behind a few businesses, and he agreed to help me."

Yep, she just called me handsome. Best day of the month. Maybe the whole year.

"Read the report when you can, Jack. I forwarded the email to you with the link to the secure document storage on the cloud. It'll ask for a password. Just put in the name of your favorite reporter and the day that you met her." She made a kissing sound into the phone, and then ended the connection.

As soon as I was parked, I hurried across the street and into my building. The wait for the elevator seemed endless, until finally a loud ding announced the arrival of a car. People spilled out, moving as slow as snails, and then I rushed in and jabbed

121

the button for my floor a few times. I almost sprinted down the hallway to unlock and open the door to my small office suite.

My laptop was quick to power up, and I logged into it and then my email program. Karen's email was at the top of the list, and I clicked to open it and find the link to the secure document site. The hardest part of the password was remembering the exact day I'd met her, when I found her leaning against my car after I'd been searching a park for Nox essence to give me a clue in the search for Penny.

I felt myself deflate as soon as I got past the password. This wasn't going to be a simple process, since I was staring at a file larger than most books I downloaded. I clicked on the file, waited for it to download and open, and then sighed. Two hundred and ninety-two pages of what looked to be dry financial analysis was revealed. I started the long process of flipping through the pages, skimming to see if I could find what had excited Karen so much.

When Nyk entered my office an hour later, I was only halfway through the document; I had to get up every fifteen minutes or so to pace the office a few times and rest my eyes, before sitting and hunching over the screen once more. He fell into an armless chair, generating a creak that sounded as if the piece of furniture were about to give up the struggle to support his weight.

I could tell from the look in his eye that his morning hadn't been any more productive than mine. "No luck with your informants?"

"Worse. I'm sure a few of them know something, but the moment I mention the Magpie their mouths stop working and they remember somewhere else they need to be. Something has these people scared, Jack, and they're not the sort to scare easily."

"All the more reason to track him down," I said, turning my attention back to the document. "Karen came by last night. She has a source that did a lot of digging into the financials behind the holding companies. Apparently, there's something interesting in here but I haven't found it yet."

The bounty hunter rose to his feet and circled my desk to bend over my shoulder. Someone so large would be expected to make the room shake as they walked, but somehow Nyk moved as silently and gracefully as a cat. Had he turned to a life of crime, I had no doubt he would have been one of the best thieves in the state. His breath was hot on the side of my face, until I nudged the laptop to the side to where he didn't have to hover so close to read the screen. The pages I was currently perusing detailed the annual income and expenditures of Pica Sericea, the holding company that had owned the retirement home on the south side.

It only took seven minutes for Nyk to find what I had skipped over while skimming the document. Buried in the corporate speak of the report was a name that repeated every few pages. That same name showed up several times in lists of shareholders or board members for the various parent corporations of holding companies. Harold Goldblatt.

"Son of a bitch," I whispered, fighting back a grin. Nyk chuckled and patted me on the shoulder. "We have a lead!"

I quickly pulled up my people search websites and typed the name into them. I had three of them running, checking city, state, and national records. The local search was always my first hope, for a narrower list of results than the state and national databases would provide. This time, I got lucky and the search brought up two results within several minutes.

The first local Harold Goldblatt was a ninety-something retiree, living in one of the many assisted living centers across town. He couldn't be ruled out, but I figured it was safe to mark him as least likely. The second result was a man in his fifties, with a large and full social media presence. The man seemed to enjoy being at parties of any kind, flashing a leering smile at any camera within ten miles of him.

He also owned a store called Goldie's Cash & Pawn, and according to the website, they specialized in paying top dollar for any gold jewelry a customer should wish to sell. Based on the heavy chains around his neck and wrists in the photos, and the many, many rings on his fingers, most of that gold ended up on his person.

I grabbed my gray herringbone and followed Nyk through the door, pausing only long enough to lock the outer door behind me. Within minutes, we were climbing into his monster truck parked half a block from my building. The store was only fifteen minutes away with light traffic, and even with the tail end of the lunch rush crowd we made it there in eighteen.

Goldie's Cash & Pawn was in an anchor spot of a small strip mall, occupying the largest space on one end. Yellow flags were strung along the roof line, over a sign proclaiming WE BUY YOUR GOLD!!!!!!! Yeah, there really were that many exclamation points. It reeked of desperation to me, but I guess if you were desperate yourself it would seem like a lifeline. The pawn side of the business seemed to be doing well, too, based on the rather nice guitars and amplifiers in the window. A couple of red riding lawnmowers were parked just outside the door, as well, with handwritten signs enticing buyers to ask for a price within.

Nyk parked a few stores away, finding a spot where we could see the entrance of Goldie's without too much trouble. "How do you want to handle this?"

I considered the location, close to a busy intersection, and couldn't help but wish this had been the sleazy store in a back alley that I'd expected. "This place is pretty exposed, so intimidation tactics aren't going to work."

He grunted, raising a hand to point out a cluster of video cameras above the store's entrance. "That's some high-end gear. Anyone willing to spend that kind of money is sure to have lots of digital eyes on the inside, as well."

"We could always try waiting until they close, jump them when they're locking up." I ran my eye along the strip mall, examining each store. There was a strange feeling tickling the back of my mind, and I couldn't figure out what it was.

"This part of town is too nice, Jack. I bet the cops cruise these streets all the time, happy to smile and wave and not worry about seeing a mugging or carjacking every day." He looked at me, raising an eyebrow. "Why don't we just walk in, ask for Harold, and see what happens?"

"Sure, we could do that. Except for the part where you're a giant and I'm the most recognized face in the Nox world. They'd warn Harold about who was looking for him, and he'd scamper or send muscle after us." Maybe it was the colors of the shopping center? It felt so maddeningly familiar, but I couldn't remember why.

"You are too much of a pessimist, my friend. They'd have to be Nox to recognize you, and there are plenty of people as tall as me in this city."

"Yeah, and they all wear black and silver uniforms eighty-two nights each season. More in a good year." He did make a good point, though. It was futile to sit and worry about whether we'd be recognized, when whoever was inside the store could turn out to be normal humans. Harold Goldblatt himself could be one, unaware that he was doing business with supernatural creatures.

So, Nyk and I got out of the truck and walked through the parking lot. I knew I should keep my attention on the store we were approaching, but I kept looking around trying to find out why this place was so familiar to me. It felt like an old memory. Maybe from the last time I was trying to find the Magpie?

Then it hit me. My sister's charge for soliciting had been in front of a blue and yellow storefront. Could she have been hanging around Goldie's in the days and weeks before she was murdered? If so, then it was even more imperative that I track

126

down this Harold Goldblatt, who was looking increasingly more likely to be a direct lead to the Magpie.

Nyk pulled open the door to Goldie's, releasing a burst of warm air from within. The day had been warmer than usual for January, but it still felt good after a walk through the chilly wind. Inside, the store had glass cases running along the three interior walls. The large open space in the middle of the store had various items set up so that customers could walk around and look at them. These were some of the higher value pawned items; a couple of expensive looking sleek white drones, a very convoluted and fancy barbecue/smoker pit, several large flat screen televisions with signs proclaiming, "still works great!!!". There was even a handful of baseball cards in protective cases, showing some of the old greats. Each of them had a signature scrawled across the player's face, and even a person like me who wasn't into baseball had to stop and gawk.

"How can I help you gentlemen today?" I looked up to see a young woman approaching with a wide smile on her face. She was wearing a marigold shirt tucked into blue slacks, an off-putting combination even though it matched the color of the storefront.

"Hi, Natali," I said, reading her name tag as she got closer. "My friend and I happened to be passing by, and thought we'd stop in and say hi to our friend Harold. Is he in?"

She stopped in her tracks, the smile slipping for a moment before it went back to full wattage. Her eyes examined us, lingering on Nyk. "I'm sorry, sir, Goldie's has several locations across town, and we even have a store in Austin now. The owner visits whenever he feels the need, and he doesn't have a set schedule."

"Sounds just like old Harold, huh?" I laughed, poking Nyk with an elbow a few times until he turned a glare on me. "Maybe I could leave my number, and you could get it to him?" I didn't give her a chance to refuse, pulling out one of the white cards with just my name and mobile number on it. She took it reluctantly, looking at it and frowning. "Great stuff in this store, by the way. So much better than the pawn shops when I was a kid, where all you'd see was tarnished silver or dirty old jewelry."

"Mr. Goldblatt runs a quality establishment," the clerk said, almost as if she'd been saying it every day for years. She probably had.

"That he does." I looked at the nearest glass case, spotting a line of gold coins. That instantly drew my attention, and I had to fight to keep my hand from straying up to grab my amulet. Coins had become an obsession with me after I received one of the Nine, as I tried to find anything that could be similar and lead me to information on where my coin came from.

The clerk noticed my attention, and her smile turned almost sharkish. She stepped forward, placed a hand on my arm to gently guide me toward the case, and waved her other hand at the display. "Are you a collector, sir? We have some of the best quality old coins in town. Some of the rarest, too. Mr. Goldblatt has been a collector of ancient coins since he was a child, and he loves seeing them find new homes."

I leaned over the case, entranced by the rows of variously sized coins. There were dollar coins from the early twentieth century sitting beside a near mint Spanish doubloon from the early days of the New World. A small coin almost hidden among them proved to be a late Roman period denarius. The case contained several thousand dollars' worth of coins, at the very least.

"A few of these coins were sold to us for the price of their gold or silver weight, if you can believe it." Natali was continuing with her sales pitch, excitement growing in her voice as she sensed the possibility that I might be interested in buying. "The Spanish doubloon is the pride of Mr. Goldblatt's collection. He loves it more than his children, but I think we could persuade him to let it go to the right buyer."

"It's a beautiful coin," I whispered, leaning in closer. In the reflection of the glass case, I could see Nyk walking to the far side of the store. I wasn't sure what he was doing, but I knew I had to keep the clerk busy. And hope that no customers came in. "How much would it take to buy that?"

"Well," Natali said, raising a hand to tap her temple as she considered what to say. "The last offer was two hundred, and Mr. Goldblatt turned it down. He did seem tempted, however, so if you could do two twenty-five, I think you could take it home."

"Two hundred dollars?" I asked in surprise at the low price.

The clerk chuckled, while giving me an appraising look that told me she was re-evaluating my potential as a buyer. "No, sir. Two hundred *thousand*."

I choked back an exclamation, staring wide eyed at the coin sitting in the case. I'd expected five or maybe even ten thousand for something so old, but never considered the price could be in the six figures. Why the hell was something so valuable not locked away in a vault somewhere? "Oh, yeah, that's a much more realistic price. I was worried it might be a knock off for a minute."

"Absolutely not!" Natali seemed angry that I'd even think such a thing. I guess I had just impugned the integrity of the store. "We offer certificates of authenticity for every coin over one hundred dollars, along with second opinion certificates for any that are worth more than a thousand. I can guarantee that you are looking at a real Spanish gold coin from the late seventeenth century."

I made a few more appreciative noises, watching Nyk's movements in the blurry reflection. I thought I was going to have to ask if I could hold the coin to stall for more time, but then saw him moving in our direction. "It's an absolute gem of a coin, Natali, one that I'd love to have in my collection. I just don't have the liquid cash at the moment to make the offer required to secure it." It all sounded like nonsense coming out of my mouth, but I'd heard people talk this way while sitting in waiting rooms at brokerage offices.

"Perhaps one of the other coins for today? Something to keep you from regretting not walking out of the store without something new for your collection."

Okay, I have to admit she was a rather good saleswoman. I almost told her I'd buy one, before I remembered I was a poor investigator who didn't have hundreds or thousands of dollars to spend on something that would sit on a shelf. "Oh, these others aren't what I'm looking for. Too common," I said, leaning in conspiratorially. "Tell Harold to call me, and we can discuss an offer on the doubloon. I'll make sure he knows you've been instrumental in piquing my interest."

Natali looked upset that she didn't get the sale, and what I was sure would be a hefty commission, but she did look down at my card again. There was more interest in her expression this time, and I felt confident that Harold Goldblatt would get the message that I'd visited. Nyk and I left the store, holding the door open for a woman bundled up in a heavy coat. Sunglasses and a fringe of dark hair obscured her face, but I could see a slash of red lips as she nodded her thanks.

"Good thinking with the coin thing," Nyk said, once we were back inside his truck.

"It was more a spur of the moment fascination," I admitted. "Did you find whatever you were looking for?"

He held up a scrap of paper with ten digits scrawled across it. "Taped to the desk under the keyboard, Goldie's private number."

"Huh," I said, plucking the piece of paper from his hand. "I guess you want people to be able to reach you when there's a coin worth two hundred grand sitting in a poorly guarded case. But what about the high-end security system? Not afraid of getting a visit from the cops when someone sees footage of you stepping behind the counter?"

Nyk shrugged. "I know people who run stores like these. They don't call the cops unless there's a problem they can't handle themselves. If anyone reviews the tapes, they'll only know we were asking for Goldblatt. By then, we'll have tracked the guy down."

"Won't be too hard," I said, reading the screen of my phone. I'd run a search on the number and got an immediate hit. "This isn't a cell phone, but an old-fashioned landline. And now I have Harold Goldblatt's home address."

THEN

During the bus ride into work, I kept reaching into the compartment of my backpack where the case with the talisman was stored. I'd had dreams about the thing all day, waking every half hour to check and make sure it was still there. I kept telling myself to stop being so stupid and paranoid, but then I'd blink, and my hand would be reaching into the backpack once more to touch the case.

I grabbed a seat at the rear of the bus, glad to find I had a few rows of privacy. After a quick glance around, I pulled the case from my bag and carefully opened the lid. The coin with the unfamiliar profile stamped onto it was still there. It seemed to emit its own light in the dimness of the city bus. I reached out to stroke the smooth metal with a finger, the electricity running through my body as it had the first time I touched it.

The bus driver slammed on the brakes unexpectedly, and I felt the coin slide forward in the case. My fingers grabbed for it almost without thought. Before I realized I was doing it, the talisman had been removed from the case and I was slipping the chain over my head. The coin fell to lay against my chest, cold even through my polo shirt. With numb fingers, I lifted it and slid it underneath the fabric. A creeping cold spread across my chest, and I had to fight a desire to rip the talisman off and throw it far away. It grew to an almost painful intensity, and I squeezed my eyes shut as I clenched my jaw to keep from crying out.

A second later, the feeling was gone. I could still feel the gold and silver coin against my skin, but it was warm now. The silver chain was so delicate and light that I almost had to touch it to realize it was still there. For all the weight I'd felt from the case, the coin seemed no heavier than a feather while hanging around my neck.

Reminded of the case, I looked around in alarm. It had fallen to the floor and was laying open several feet in front of me. I quickly stooped down to grab it and watched a small bit of white paper flutter down. I grabbed it before it could hit the ground. It was a piece of cocktail napkin, with splotched writing from getting wet before or after someone decided to use it for a note. LYON'S DEN were the only words I could make out, and I wasn't entirely sure I'd gotten the first word right. Shouldn't that be *lion's* den? Maybe someone trying to arrange a meeting at the zoo?

I kept studying the napkin fragment until the bus reached the stop for my job. Having come up with nothing else from the few other smudged letters or numbers, I shoved it into a pocket and slung my backpack over my shoulder. Maybe I could figure it out during my "lunch" break around two a.m. If not, it could wait. I planned to track down the place my sister had received the warning for soliciting, see if I could ask around and find anyone who might have known her.

The amulet was almost forgotten as I settled in at the desk I shared and got to work. I barely remembered I had it, except for the times it would bump against my chest after sitting back from a hunched over position I had the bad habit of adopting while talking on the phone. Each time, I would reach up to feel it and run my fingers over the contours through my shirt. Then I'd catch myself zoning out, and feel like Bilbo Baggins stroking his ring.

The second time it happened, I thought about taking the amulet off and sliding it into my backpack, stashed under my desk. Just the thought made my hands shaky and I felt nervous all of a sudden. Once I decided against it, my body returned to normal. If my work phone hadn't started to ring at that moment, I would have done some serious wondering about what the hell I was wearing.

Later in the evening, I was sitting at a table in the company break room munching on my bologna sandwich and off brand potato chips. The napkin fragment was laying on the table in front of me, but I was focused on feeling the amulet through my shirt. "Lyon's Den? Isn't that the bar downtown?" A voice startled me, drawing me back to reality.

I looked up to see a scruffy older man leaning against the table. "Bar? Do you know where it is?"

He laughed, shaking his head and pulling a chip from a bag to stuff in his mouth. "Riverwalk, I'm pretty sure. I remember reading about it in some article a few years ago. 'Best bars and restaurants you've never visited' or something like that. You got a hot date tomorrow night?"

"No, why do you ask?"

A crumb-covered finger pointed at the napkin scrap. "I thought that said *8 PM, Sat.* That's tomorrow night. Well, technically tonight now."

I squinted at the napkin. Expecting those specific letters, I thought he might be right. I felt a shiver run down my spine as I thought about the fact that the day on the napkin would be the very one after I got the parcel with the amulet and notes in it. There was no specific date, of course, so this could have meant the following Saturday. Or three weeks earlier. But it was a start. I just needed to find this bar, and then wait to see if someone showed up looking for a person they were supposed to meet.

After work and several hours of sleep at the shelter, the nice ladies that volunteered there gave me a send-off with home-baked oatmeal cookies. I would have preferred chocolate chip or snickerdoodle, but there was no way I was going to turn down free cookies. It made me all the more distressed about having to leave and find a new place to sleep, though.

By midafternoon, I was exiting a bus downtown. It was only a block to the first set of stairs that led to the Riverwalk below the street level. Saturday afternoons in summer, the Riverwalk is a tourist mecca. That day it was so crowded I could barely move at a snail's pace because of the crush of people walking the narrow path. It always amazed me that so many people could pass each other without someone being bumped off into the shallow water of the river.

I made two loops of the downtown Riverwalk, checking every sign for the words Lyon's Den. The first time around I thought I must have missed it, or it was hidden behind a pack of tourists. I moved slower the second trip and still couldn't spot anything close to being the place I was looking for. I even stopped and asked a couple of hostesses standing outside restaurants if they could direct me. That earned only blank looks in return before they started in on how their establishment served top quality drinks and I need look no further.

I probably would have given up the search then, but a homeless woman was sitting near the last hostess stand I stopped to ask directions at. As I walked away feeling defeated, she started to cackle. "What would someone like you want to find the Den for?"

It took me a few seconds to realize she was speaking in my direction, and I'm sure I only caught it because the word Den was so heavily on my mind that afternoon. I got as close as I could bear and crouched down. "Do you know where it is? I'm, uh, meeting someone there."

She stopped laughing and looked at me hard, squinting her eyes. The woman looked old at a glance, but close up I could see that she was probably no more than forty. A life on the streets was hard enough to make anyone age faster. "You don't belong there, primate. Only the Children are welcome at the Den."

Great, dozens of homeless people panhandling the tourist traps, and I get the one who's obviously out of her mind. "I'm not sure what children you mean. The Lyon's Den is a bar, right?"

The homeless woman cackled again, raising a finger to stab at my chest. "Foolish primate. You don't even know enough to be afraid." She laughed louder, looking around at the people passing by trying to avoid eye contact. "Look for the sign of the leprechaun. When you see it, look to your right and take five steps down. That is the entrance to the Den. Now go!" She waved me away, pointing in the direction I should go.

I didn't wait for her to spout more crazy things. I was tempted to ignore her words, put them down as the product of an obviously broken mind, but I figured I might as well be sure. No point in spending three hours roaming around only to leave and wonder later if her directions might have worked.

The mention of a leprechaun confused me, until I approached the sign for an Irish pub restaurant ten minutes later. I'd seen the sign twice already that afternoon, and this was the first time I saw the little pot of gold in the bottom corner of it. Did I immediately stop and turn? Or keep going until I was directly under the sign? I chose a cautious path and looked to my right as I walked.

Only a few seconds later I saw five steps leading down. They were gray stone and looked older than anything else in the city. The center of each step was worn down in a shallow groove from generations of feet following them down to where overhanging vines tried to hide a dumpster and two steel doors. One was shiny silver, and the sign on it clearly stated it was only meant for employees of the Irish pub. The other was painted a slate gray and almost blended in with the wall. There was no sign on or near it, and the pull handle looked rusty as if it were rarely used. I stood in the small space considering both doors. I wondered briefly why the homeless woman didn't mention which door to choose, but then realized I was lucky she'd been coherent at all considering all the other wacky things she'd spouted off. Shrugging, I reached out and pulled open the gray door.

The handle was surprisingly smooth, not flaking off bits of paint and rust as it had appeared. It was pleasantly cool in contrast to the summer heat. The door was heavy, but it swung open on smooth hinges. I had almost expected an exaggerated creaking like you hear in horror movies, but it was completely silent. The interior of the bar was too dim to make out much detail, especially for eyes accustomed to the bright afternoon.

I took a deep breath and stepped inside, letting the door swing shut behind me. The thud of it made me cringe, wondering if I'd just drawn too much attention to myself. I waited a few steps inside for half a minute, letting my eyes adjust to the darkness. There were none of the garish neon signs advertising beer brands that I was accustomed to seeing at bars I visited with my friends in previous years. The air wasn't filled with country music or older rock songs, either. Instead there was a steady hum that was somehow pleasant to listen to.

"This works better if you take a seat," a voice said, giving me a jolt. I realized my eyes had closed, and when I opened them, I was able to see a man behind a long wooden bar. He looked to be in his early forties, with reddish-brown hair grown long enough to sweep back from his high forehead. There was a healthy tan on his skin, something I'd come to wonder about in the months and years to come. He stood a few inches taller than my six feet, lanky but exuding a sense of strength. The man wiped a white rag across the bar top in front of him, gesturing for me to take the stool there.

"I'm, uh, looking for a place called Lyon's Den. Is this it?"

"You've found it, friend. My name is Richard Lyon, owner and bartender." As soon as I was settled on the soft leather stool with my backpack at my feet, he pulled a tall glass from behind the bar and examined me. "You have the look of a beer man, not a fan of the stronger drinks. I'm betting you usually order one of those mass-produced corporate concoctions, am I right?"

"Um, yeah," I said, feeling uneasy with the situation. This place was unlike any other bar I'd ever been in before, even aside from the lack of the usual décor. There was a feel to the place that was like standing too close to a high voltage power line. It felt like every hair on my body was standing up, but when I looked at my arms that wasn't the case.

"I just got a batch of special blackberry lager from a local microbrewery. Only ten kegs produced, and I managed to get a couple. You're going to enjoy this." He pulled on the tap to fill the glass, then turned and set the beer in front of me. I opened my mouth to point out that I hadn't ordered anything, but he just motioned for me to drink.

The beer was pleasantly cold, making me realize I'd been sweating most of the afternoon and was overheated. I was prepared to pretend enjoyment of the drink, but I was surprised to find that I loved the slightly sweet flavor of the blackberry beer. I took a few more deep drinks before setting the half-full glass down on the bar. "That's pretty good stuff," I admitted. "I, uh, don't really have cash to pay for this, though." I felt myself going red with the embarrassment of the situation.

"First one's on the house," the bartender said, waving his rag. "All I ask is that you tell me what brought you in. Don't take this the wrong way, but you're not the type of person that usually comes through that door."

I hadn't planned on telling him anything, but there was a charm about the man that made me decide to open up. Maybe the fact that we were the only two people in the bar helped, as well. I told him about my sister's death and the package she left for me, without mentioning what was in it, and then showed him the napkin fragment. "It's the only real clue I have to help me find out what Jen was doing the last couple of months. This place was very hard to find, by the way. You should put a sign by the door or something."

"I'll consider it," Richard said with a slight smirk, appearing through the astonishment that had been growing with each word of my story. "I'm truly sorry to hear that your sister is dead. You said Jen. Does that mean your sister was Jennifer Dahlish?"

Hearing her name from his lips made me gasp in surprise. "Yes! Did you know her?"

He sighed, leaning against the bar and tossing the white rag to hang over his shoulder. "You must be Jack, then. Jennifer became a regular the last few weeks. You're actually sitting in

141

her favorite spot," he said with a smile. "She always said she could see the entire room from there and keep an eye on the others."

"Others? Did she come here with friends? Could you give me names so I could reach out and ask them questions?"

"No, I wouldn't say friends," Richard said, sounding uncertain of how to explain. "How much do you know about what your sister has been doing?"

"I don't know anything," I moaned. "She ran away from our apartment in April, and aside from a very short call a few weeks later I haven't heard from her at all. Can you tell me anything about it?"

"Well, I'm not sure how much I should say. She got mixed up with some pretty dangerous people, Jack. Do you really want to risk falling foul of that kind of crowd?"

I took another drink of the beer, moistening my suddenly dry mouth. "I might have already," I said, going on to tell him about the encounter with Billy Wish in the club, and the beating that followed.

Richard scowled as he listened. "This is what happens when one of the Nine isn't claimed," he muttered. The words confused me, and I was about to ask what he meant when he shook his head and slapped a hand on the bar. "I don't know this Billy character, but I know the reputation of that club. Shine. You really shouldn't have ever set foot in a place like that, Jack. It's not meant for humans."

"What? Only aliens?" I asked, laughing and trying to figure out if everyone on the Riverwalk had picked today to go crazy.

"They've been confused for them before." Richard stood and grabbed my glass, which I'd somehow emptied without realizing it. He stepped over to the tap to fill it again. "I hate to be the one to shatter your view of the world, Jack Dahlish, but I'm going to tell you something I think you have a right to know."

He set the full glass down in front of me, pulling the rag from this shoulder to wipe away a few drops of condensation that had fallen from it. "Monsters are real," he said, raising his eyes to meet mine. "Every fairy tale or ghost story you heard as a kid, every campfire tale about creatures lurking in the dark, all of that is true. Well, based on truth. Those things really do exist, though they can look just like you and me when they want to. You could work with one, or live next to one, and never know it."

I was leaning back on my stool as he spoke, reaching down to grab my backpack. Whatever was in the water around here, I didn't want to catch it. "Okay, good to know. Thanks for that. I think I need to get going. Think about that sign."

My hand was on the push bar to exit when Richard's word stopped me. "What was in that package, Jack?" I didn't turn, trying to force myself to keep going forward and walk away from all the madness of the last half hour. Get back to my normal life and never think of the lunacy again.

"Your sister was working as a courier for someone called the Magpie, Jack. Whatever was in that package, his people are going to be looking for it. I think you deserve to know what's coming after you."

In those few sentences, I learned more about my sister's life of the last several months than in all my weeks of searching and trying to find answers. I still wanted to leave and forget the entire day had happened, but I knew it would be impossible now. I turned away from the door and climbed back onto the stool, dropping my backpack at my feet. "Who is this Magpie?" I asked. "Some kind of drug dealer, who talked my sister into carrying his filth around?"

Richard gave me a pitying look, one that made me bristle in prideful defiance. It wasn't until weeks later that I realized he was mourning the loss of my innocence. "The Magpie doesn't deal in drugs. He, or she, no one knows for sure, buys things. Important things, and sometimes seemingly unimportant. It doesn't really matter what the items are most of the time, as long as it has value to the person it belongs to. That's what makes the Magpie want it. And occasionally, he or she sells items to others. That's a rare thing, though, in my experience."

"What did my sister do for this person? Carry the items being bought and sold?"

"Exactly. Jennifer would be given a time and a place, where she would meet one of the Magpie's agents. An item would be passed off, and it was her job to carry it to the next link in the chain. I've heard it said that there are only a handful of people in the world who know the Magpie's real identity, because of this long series of go-betweens."

It was astounding that my sister could have fallen in with this kind of operation. "This Billy Wish kid must be a Magpie agent or something. Her friends said Jen started to go off without them after meeting him at Shine, and that was only a few weeks before she left our place."

Richard nodded. "It wouldn't surprise me, based on what you told me. Rumors have always put that club as part of the Magpie's holdings. It's one of the reasons I said you should never have gone there. I told Jennifer the same thing, but she just said it was an exciting place to be. Especially once she knew what it really was."

"A link in a black-market chain?"

"No, one of the havens for Nox."

And here came the crazy train again. "Nitrous oxide? Is it a hangout for street racers or something?"

Richard laughed, looking around as if wishing he had someone to share the joke with. "No, Jack. Nox are the monsters I told you about. Filii Nox, or the Children of Darkness. I could go on for hours, but we'll save that for when you come back. Short version, the universe was created by an energy force called Chaos. That same energy formed the first gods, who then broke off pieces of themselves to form other creatures as their children. These were the first Nox. They couldn't procreate as fast as humans did, though, and were eventually overrun and had to adapt to survive. These days they wear human masks to blend in with the rest of the world. Some places, like

Shine and Lyon's Den, are areas where they are welcomed and allowed to relax those disguises for a while, now and then."

Well, the homeless woman's comment about children suddenly made sense. At least, it did if you shared the delusion she and the bartender seemed to be under. "You expect me to believe that elves and dwarves and all that nonsense really exist, and they're just really good at playing hide and seek?"

"You don't have to believe it," he said with a smile. "You don't have to believe in the rain, either, but that won't stop it from falling out of the sky. The Nox are real, Jack. That's all that matters."

My dad had told me once when I was a kid that the best way to handle crazy people is to just go along with whatever they say. I remembered it so vividly because we'd been riding a city bus in San Diego when some unkempt woman stood up and started walking the aisle ranting and raving about the government persecuting her. I figured this was a similar situation. "Okay, sure, so fairies and all that are real. How does that get me closer to finding out what happened to my sister?"

Richard glared at me, obviously seeing through my pathetic attempt at placation. "Jack, what I'm telling you is that it's dangerous to pursue this any further. The Magpie is a bad person to get on the wrong side of, and you're not prepared in any way for whatever could be coming. My advice would be to dump that package with someone who can get it back to the Magpie, and hope they leave you alone after that."

I thought about his words, my hand straying to touch the amulet through my shirt as I considered the possibility of giving it up and having to live with the knowledge that I'd never find my sister's killer. That was something I couldn't do. I'd never be able to live with myself if I did.

He was watching my hand, his brow furrowed. "What was in that package, Jack? Was it a necklace?"

I jerked my hand away from it. "Yeah. So what?"

Richard pinched the bridge of his nose, and I heard a growl of frustration. "You pulled a necklace out of a parcel that could have come from anywhere, and just stuck it around your neck?"

"There was a note from Jen," I protested. "I didn't exactly decide to put it on. There was this bus driver, and he hit the brakes, and I grabbed the amulet to keep it from sliding to the ground, and the next thing I knew it was around my neck." I stopped, breathless, aware that I was rambling defensively.

"What does it look like?"

My mouth opened to reply, but then I felt a tickle of paranoia in the back of my mind. "Why? What does that matter?"

"I'm trying to help you, Dahlish. Is it a coin, with the face of a man on both sides? Attached to a silver chain?"

"Yes," I said quietly, looking down at where it lay under the t-shirt I was wearing. The lump of the coin was prominent under the band logo. I realized then that I had never flipped the coin over to look on the reverse side. Did it really show the same profile? *Only one way to find out*, I thought as I reached to pull it out.

Richard's hand slapped down over mine. "Don't ever take it out when people are around, or if there's a chance of being seen." His eyes were wary even as his tone was calm and measured. "If that necklace is what I think it is, then you just jumped into the deep end of the pool. You won't have the option of turning your back and forgetting all about the supernatural world lurking under the veneer of normality."

"What is it?" I asked, feeling a little frightened now. I remembered the first wave of caution when I opened the case, forgotten so soon after. Now I was hesitant to even touch the amulet.

"It has to be," he said, and I could tell he was talking to himself more than me. "There's nothing else like it, and I've never heard of anyone being foolish enough to produce copies. I'd need to see it to be sure, but I don't dare let it be exposed. Not here." Richard sighed deeply, rubbing a hand over his face.

"Jack, what you are wearing is not just a necklace. It's a whole new life. That amulet is one of the Nine, called that for the obvious reason that only nine of them exist in the world." His hand reached out, as if to touch the amulet through my shirt, and he jerked it back. "It's what we call a Relic."

I could hear the capital R in the way he said it, and it sparked a memory of Jen's note which I reached down to pull from my backpack. "That's what my sister called it," I said, passing him the note to read.

Richard read it quickly, his eyes darting across the page. "I never gave you the credit you deserved, Jennifer." He shook his head and handed the not back to me. "Your sister did a very brave thing, but now I'm certain it got her killed. The Magpie must have gotten his hands on one of the Nine somehow. That never should have happened."

148

"You still haven't explained what a Relic is, or what this necklace is supposed to be."

"A Relic is an item that has been imbued with some of the Chaos energy left over from the creation of the universe. It still flows through everything, and now and then decides to attach to certain people or things. No one has ever been able to determine if there is an intelligence behind it or if it just happens by chance.

"That amulet, and the eight others like it, are some of the oldest Relics in existence. Some of the strongest, too, from what I've seen." He shrugged, picking up the white rag once again and wiping at the bar. "As to what it does, all I can say is that it gives the wearer the ability to detect Nox. Everyone who wears one of the Nine becomes a protector in one way or another. Whether you view that as protecting the Nox from humanity or the other way around is up to your individual viewpoint."

Now I felt real apprehension. Was I seriously supposed to believe that some magical energy filled the world and imbued things with abilities? It sounded like the Force, but a lot less useful. "Look, I don't think I'm the right person to be wearing this thing if what you're saying is even close to the truth. I don't even really care about other people, aside from my sister. Why don't you tell me how I can contact one of these magic police or whatever? Maybe they can help me find my sister's killer."

"Jack, if the coin let you put it on, then you are definitely the right person to be wearing it." Richard gave me a sad smile, and it was enough to start me scrabbling with the chain. As soon as I wrapped my fingers around it and started to pull, the coin seemed to grow a hundred times heavier. It refused to move, even as I strained with all of my might against it.

The bartender pulled out an old pocket watch, snapping it open to check the time. "Look, my usual crowd is about to show up. I don't think you're ready to actually meet Nox, so maybe you should come back in the morning. We'll talk more about all of this, and I'll try to explain anything you still have questions about."

I ignored him, still straining with the delicate silver chain. It felt so fragile, as if it should have broken the first time I exerted any force on it. But it never did, even as the coin began to feel heavier and heavier until I could feel my back bowing under the pressure. When I gave up in frustration, the weight disappeared within moments. If nothing else had, that started to convince me that everything I'd learned in the Den could be true.

Just as I was about to ask more questions, the door was pulled open to emit a bright shaft of sunlight. A stoop shouldered man entered the bar, looking at me curiously before sitting at a stool seven spaces away, just around the corner of the L-shaped bar. Richard nodded amiably. "Terrance, give me a minute to finish with this gentleman and I'll get your drink."

"Go," he said quietly, turning back to me. "Think about everything I've said and come back tomorrow morning. And whatever you do, don't let anyone see it." I was on the verge of protesting when the door opened yet again, and two more patrons came in. They were laughing in loud braying voices, and for a moment I felt sure I'd turn to see non-humans. Their faces were lumpy and ugly, but no less human than my own.

I decided to follow the bartender's advice and grabbed my backpack. I took a few steps toward the door and turned quickly when I felt eyes on me. The man called Terrance was looking at me, but his attention seemed to be focused on my chest instead of my face. His brow was furrowed, and he looked as if he were confused and trying to figure something out. It took all my willpower not to reach up and wrap the coin in a protective hand as I quickly left the bar.

<u>NOW</u>

Nyk and I sat outside the house for more than three hours before we saw a car turn into the drive. If I'm being honest, it was exactly the kind of car I'd expect someone who owned a string of pawn shops to be driving. It was a late sixties Cadillac Coupe De Ville, lovingly cared for and painted the most god-awful color of baby vomit yellow I'd ever seen. I was guessing it was supposed to make you think of gold, what with the name and his chain of stores, but it was a few shades darker than it should have been for that.

We watched the rumbling car park in front of the modest two-story home. Once the engine shut off, the sudden silence was almost deafening. The door creaked open with a sound that only classic cars could make, and a large man climbed out of it. He was easily three hundred pounds, and very little of it looked to be muscle from where I was sitting. The garish yellow and green Hawaiian shirt he was wearing looked big enough to be a sail on a small boat. A straw boater was covering his salt and pepper hair, protecting his eyes from the winter sun. He was smoking a fat cigar, completing the cliché trifecta for shady pawn shop owner. It was like he'd been sent over from central casting.

"This doesn't look like a guy who owns a chain of pawn and gold shops," Nyk said.

"Or a two hundred-thousand-dollar Spanish doubloon," I agreed. "Maybe he bought it all on credit and is one of those rich people who really aren't worth much."

"At least he lives on a quiet street. I haven't seen anyone stirring in the houses nearby."

"No, but it's getting close to quitting time. I bet we see a lot of people returning home in the next half hour or so." I reached out to grab the door handle, preparing to skydive out of the monster truck to reach the street. "Let's get it done."

Nyk looked both ways before crossing the street, jogging across as if he'd seen a car on the way. I strolled slowly behind, shaking my head. If I was driving a car and saw Nyk in the middle of the road, I'd slam on the brakes so I didn't total my car on the mountain of a man.

Goldblatt's door was already open as we walked up his driveway. I was surprised to see the man leaning against the frame, puffing on his cigar with a shit-eating grin on his face. "Well, well, well. If it isn't the famous Jack Dahlish, one of the Nine. I heard you were looking for me over at my flagship store." His Texas drawl was a sharp contrast to his Miami mafia looks.

I did my best to keep my astonishment from showing. I opened my senses for a second, checking for any kind of Nox essence from Goldblatt, but could find nothing. He was as human as could be, and it was rare to find people like him who knew about the coin holders even if they were aware of the Nox. He didn't even bat an eye when he looked at Nyk towering over us both.

"Mr. Goldblatt," I said, reaching out to shake his clammy hand. "Sorry for tracking you down like this, but we have a couple of questions we were hoping you could answer."

"Call me Goldie, everyone does. C'mon in, fellas. You want a margarita? I'm making a pitcher." Nyk chuckled as we entered the house, where the heat was set much higher than I liked. I pulled off my herringbone coat and folded it over an arm, already breaking into a sweat. The house looked like it had been transplanted straight from the eighties. The décor was very heavy on wicker furniture and palm tree wallpaper. It reminded me of visiting older relatives when I was a kid, and for some reason I flashed on a memory of sitting on a green couch covered in plastic while I pushed a motorcycle toy across the cushion.

"Thank you, Goldie." I called, staring around at the living room. "Nothing for us."

"Speak for yourself," Nyk grumbled. "I'll take a margarita! Extra tequila."

"Ah, a man after my own heart. I think you'll like the way I mix them. Almost as strong as you." Goldie breezed out of the kitchen carrying two large cocktail glasses filled to the salt covered brim. The glass was so large it appeared almost normal size in Nyk's giant hand. The bounty hunter took a sip, and then broke into a wide grin of approval.

"Now, how can I help you boys?"

Sensing that my partner was going to be too busy with his drink for a while, I took the lead. "We're trying to find someone, and during our investigation we came across some of their business holdings. Looking deeper into that, we found that you were listed as a shareholder or board member for all of the main holding companies. I was hoping that you'd be able to tell us where we could find the person we're searching for."

Goldie sat in a wicker chair with a thick cushion, waving for us to take seats on the couch opposite. "Well, now, it sounds like you might be searching for a friend of mine. I'm not sure how I'd feel about providing information for something like that. Why are you looking for this person?"

Nyk was licking salt from his lips and looked about to answer, but I held up a hand. "You obviously know who I am, which must mean you know *what* I am. I think that should be enough of an answer, don't you?"

He eyed me for a bit, and the room was silent except for the slurping sounds of Nyk finishing his margarita. He belched and set the empty glass on an oak coffee table. "You want another one, son?" Goldie asked. "I've never seen anyone gulp one down that fast."

"I'm good, sir. Thank you. I'm driving."

Goldie winked and laughed, taking a sip of his margarita. "I tell you what, boys. I think I have a pretty good idea who it is you're looking for, so I'll give you a little free advice. Forget about it. Just head on home, let whoever you're working for know that you can't help them, and go back to whatever else you were working on before this came up." He turned his gaze on Nyk, seeming to convey something with his eyes. "Your employer might be very grateful if you do that, Mr. Walsh."

155

"We can't do that," I told him. "I don't know how much you know about me, but the person we're looking for had a hand in my past. And it's not the kind of thing I'm going to be able to forget or forgive. We'll find the Magpie, one way or another. If you help us, that just might be a little less messy than the other way."

Goldie chortled, crossing one leg over another and throwing an arm across the back of his chair. "You should be careful where you use that name, Mr. Dahlish. It has a power, in its own way, and you wouldn't want to call it down on yourself."

I looked at Nyk, wondering if we were going to have to get rough with Goldblatt, after all. He seemed to read my expression. "I like him, Jack. I don't think I could hit him."

"You wouldn't get anything out of it, anyway," Goldie said, rising to his feet. "Now, if you boys don't mind, I'm going to go finish off this pitcher. You can show yourselves out. Good luck now, y'hear?" He strode from the room as if he had not a care in the world, and I could only sit and stare with open-mouthed wonder.

Nyk nudged me, pointing at the seat Goldie had occupied. A business card was laying there, looking as if it had dropped from the man's pocket. I looked back to the kitchen, making sure he wouldn't reappear suddenly, and then walked over to snatch the card and stuff it in my pocket. "Come on," I said quietly, motioning for Nyk to follow as I threw on my coat and left the house.

Once we were back in the monster truck, I pulled the card out and read what was printed there. It gave the name of a lawyer, listing his office address and three phone numbers. I'd never heard of the man, but he obviously wanted to make sure that people could reach him if they needed to hire him. According to the back of the card, he specialized in financial law and had a long list of corporate clients.

"That's interesting," Nyk said after I passed the card over so he could read it. "I wonder if Goldie dropped it on purpose, a 'helping us without helping us' kind of thing."

"Don't get too fond of the guy just because he gave you alcohol. Which I could smell from the opposite end of the couch by the way. That thing must have been ninety percent tequila. You safe to drive?"

He snorted and started the truck without bothering to answer. I knew my head would have been spinning after that much alcohol, but Nyk seemed to suffer no effects at all. Leaving the middle-class neighborhood, he turned the truck south for downtown. By some weird quirk of fate, the lawyer had an office in my building.

"If this guy turns out to have information, I'm going to be a little irked that he was eight floors over my head the entire time."

It took forever to get back downtown, since we were fighting evening rush hour the entire way. Everyone going our direction seemed intent on slowing us down as much as possible, and for a long stretch we were inching forward. As we passed a wreck in the opposite lanes that had caused the rubberneck slowdown, I could only hope our lawyer worked late hours and would still be available. I thought about calling, but I didn't

157

want to risk alerting him. If Goldie had known who I and Nyk were, it was entirely possible this lawyer would as well. Especially if he was connected to the Magpie in some way.

A spot right in front of the building opened up as we approached, and Nyk was able to pull his truck into the space. It was a tight fit, but I was too impatient to think about how we might be inconveniencing the people in front and behind. I almost ran into the building, and the elevator door was opening as Nyk came through the glass doors of the lobby. Once the elevator emptied, we shoved into it and I pressed the button for the lawyer's floor.

The doors opened to reveal a lavishly decorated reception area, with dark cherry wood furniture and several oil paintings on the wall that looked like they cost more than I made in a year. Okay, probably more like five years. I'm definitely not rolling in the dough with my job.

A young woman with a nice headset sitting on top of her black hair looked up and smiled the smile of receptionists everywhere. She pressed a button to mute her microphone and said, "How can I help you gentlemen this evening?"

"Hi, we're here to see Morris Chatterton. We were referred to him by another client." I gave her my best smile, trying to charm my way in.

It didn't work. "Do you have an appointment with Mr. Chatterton?"

"No. My friend assured me he would see us. Tell him we're here about Pica Hudsonia."

"Take a seat and I'll see if Mr. Chatterton is in, please." The receptionist unmuted her microphone and began talking to whoever was on the line.

Nyk and I sat in leather wingback chairs, flanking a table covered in magazines. I pushed them around, looking at titles like *Yachting Monthly* and *Sur La Terre*. This law firm was definitely not a place I'd ever end up if I found myself in legal trouble. I wasn't sure I'd be able to afford two minutes talking to the overpriced suits I expected to find if we made it out of reception.

"I'm sorry, gentlemen, Mr. Chatterton has already left for the day. If you'd like, I can schedule some time with you at his next available opening." The receptionist's tone had a bit of frost in it now, and I felt certain that whoever she had spoken to made it clear we weren't welcome. I wondered at that until I looked up and noticed several discreet camera lenses covering the room.

"No, thank you. I'm sure we'll run into old Morris soon enough on our own." I grinned, grabbed one of the expensive magazines, and sauntered to the elevator. Sure, it was a petty move, but it made me feel better.

Nyk was right behind me, holding his arms over his chest and looking all the world like he was hired muscle. The door opened with a ding. After we filed in, I waved at the reception-ist who was now glaring daggers at us.

"So now what?" Nyk asked once the elevator doors closed.

"Now we wait," I said. "I'm quite sure our Mr. Chatterton was still in the office, or the young lady would have told us he was away when I first asked to meet with him." The elevator doors slid open to reveal the marbled glory of the lobby. "The building has a back entrance, but I can't see a high-priced lawyer walking through a filthy alley. We'll stake out the main door and wait for him to leave."

It was full dark, and traffic had trickled down to almost nothing, by the time I saw Chatterton leave the building. As soon as we were in the truck, I'd scoured social media sites and the law firm's own website to find pictures of the man until I was sure I'd recognize him. He looked a lot like JFK, with a face that instantly spoke of East Coast privilege. It made me wonder if his voice would carry the same nasally accent.

I'd expected the lawyer to cross the street to the open-air parking lot where I always left my car, or perhaps to the garage next to it, and had told Nyk to park facing them. Instead, Chatterton stepped to the curb and a black car that had just parked a few feet away ten minutes earlier pulled around the car in front of it. The driver got as close to the curb as he could, then rushed to exit the car and circle around to hold a door for the lawyer.

The car pulled away from the curb, and I thought for a second that we'd have to pull a U-turn to follow. But the black car executed the maneuver instead, sliding past us smoothly during a break in the traffic. Nyk started the monster truck and followed, keeping a large gap between us. I would have preferred tailing the lawyer in my Honda, a car that's easy to get lost in among even a small amount of traffic, but I wasn't sure the bounty hunter could have fit even if we somehow removed a front seat.

"I've got twenty that says he's going home," Nyk said.

"You're on. My gut is telling me we spooked him by mentioning one of the shell companies. I bet he's going to meet one of the Magpie's agents. Maybe Mr. Magpie himself."

"Your gut is telling you it's hungry," he said, a statement I couldn't dispute as a gurgling sound filled the cab of the truck. I'd vetoed the idea of picking up some food to eat during our little stakeout, and breakfast had been a long time ago.

"My gut's telling me we're losing him," I said, pointing to where the black car was making a turn a few blocks ahead. Nyk had to press on the gas to get through a yellow light, but we made the turn soon enough to see the car take another down the street. "Where are they going? There's nothing in that direction but the warehouse district."

I was feeling even more baffled ten minutes later, when Nyk cut the lights and coasted to a stop a couple of blocks from where the black car had parked at the curb. We'd made the final turn in just enough time to see the lawyer disappearing through a door, which closed behind him and cut off the wan light from within.

"Son of a bitch," I said. "We came from a different direction than I'm used to, or I would have noticed sooner. That's the building where Shine used to be!"

Nyk pointed to where two people wearing coats with concealing hoods were approaching the building from the opposite

161

direction. Once they reached the door, one of them held it open and then followed the other inside.

"The Magpie might be in there," I said excitedly. "Think about it. Chatterton gets freaked out when we mention one of the shell companies, and checks the cameras. Maybe he recognizes me, maybe he sends our photos off to someone else who does. People start freaking out, asking how we got so deep into things, and they plan a meet to discuss it." Nyk didn't look too convinced when I glanced over. "Look, we'll go double or nothing on that bet. I'll sneak around back, find some way into the building, and just take a look. If it looks like a shady meeting, I'll call and we can decide what to do."

He was shaking his head the entire time, but I could see I was going to win. I slid out of my gray herringbone, not wanting anything to happen to the expensive coat while I was scaling walls or shimmying through windows. Luckily, I'd worn a black t-shirt for the day. That and my dark blue jeans would keep me hidden in the shadows so I could sneak around better.

"If I'm not back or calling you in thirty...."

"Don't worry. I'll call the cops, or the National Guard."

"Fuck no. Come in and save me."

THEN

I had a lot to think about after my visit to the Lyon's Den, and I rode a city bus for a few hours until my night shift started. I kept replaying the conversation in my head, trying to figure out how much I should believe and how much was unadulterated insanity. The bartender had seemed certain of what he was saying, but so did the guy I'd passed on the street one day talking about how the lizard people were wearing human masks to infiltrate and take over our government.

In the end, I decided to shelve the matter until after another eight hours of taking calls and doing mindless data entry. The more pressing concern was where I'd sleep the next day. I'd receive my first paycheck for this job at the end of the night's shift, so maybe I could think about springing for a cheap motel room somewhere. The thought of a private room and bathroom was the height of luxury after more than a month of sleeping on friend's couches and then in the shelter.

That fantasy lasted through the night, until a little after three in the morning when my supervisor breezed past and dropped an envelope on my desk. I was almost rubbing my hands with glee as I sliced it open and pulled out the check within. My ecstatic grin slipped as soon as I saw the depressingly low amount. The check was for the first half of the month, and I'd taken three days off after my sister's body was found.

Attempting to stay positive, I knew I didn't have any bills other than my huge hospital debt and my cell phone. I could deposit it all in my bank account, adding it to the twenty-seven cent fortune that currently occupied it, and start thinking about how to rebuild my life. As much as the job frustrated me, so far I seemed to be doing it well enough that I didn't have to worry about coming in to find a pink slip on my desk one evening. The woman who sat there during the day shift had even started leaving me little inspirational notes, stuck to the monitor or tucked inside a drawer. It surprised me how emotional I became when I found the first one, giving me a sense of camaraderie that I'd missed.

By the time I exited the building into pre-dawn stillness, I was feeling better about my situation than I had in months. A little internet research had provided two leads for men's shelters that were only one or two bus transfers from my work. I'd been unable to call because of the early hours, but they'd be open by the time I stopped in and check on the possibility of getting a bed for another week or two. Hopefully by then I'd have enough saved to spring for a deposit on a cheap apartment, or maybe find someone looking for a roommate.

Seven of my co-workers waited at the bus stop with me. Most of them were in a little group chatting away, people who rode the same bus to and from work every day. I felt a little envious of them. It had been far too long since I'd been able to go out for a night at a bar or club with my friends. Thinking about it, I realized the last time I'd done such a thing was the last night in Shine. I shuddered at the memory, and thought that it might not be such a bad thing to stay away from clubs for a while longer.

My bus was the fourth one to arrive at the stop, and I was glad to climb the steps and slump into an empty seat near the middle. I leaned against the window, fighting the droopiness of my eyelids as my body was telling me it needed rest. A shuddering jolt as the bus pulled away from a later stop woke me from a light doze, and I looked around as I tried to rub the tiredness from my eyes.

Two rows ahead of me was a familiar head of spiky brown hair. I tried to convince myself I was being paranoid, but then the man turned to the side and I saw the beak of a nose and weak chin. It was the same man who'd been observing me on the bus a few days earlier. The same day I'd received the parcel with the coin and my sister's note. I knew I was letting the insanity I'd heard in the bar the previous evening get to me, but I couldn't shake the feeling that he was following me.

We were still several stops from the first shelter on my list to visit, but as soon as the bus pulled up to the curb for the next stop I jumped out of my seat and almost sprinted off. I started walking down the street, looking over my shoulder to see if the man would follow, and breathed a sigh of relief when he didn't. I also felt like a total fool as I turned and walked back to the bus stop to wait for the next bus going to my destination. My paranoia had just cost me ten or fifteen minutes.

The first shelter was full, and the man inside the door was apologetic. He explained that I wouldn't have qualified for their facility, anyway, based on the paycheck I'd received. That particular shelter was funded by government grants and required no income or one lower than the pittance I was pulling in with my new job. Looking around at all the people shuffling through the hall, I would have felt terrible if I had taken a bed from one of them.

Half an hour later, I struck out at the second shelter. It turned out to be a very small facility, with room for only a dozen people each evening. They didn't allow anyone inside during daytime hours, which meant I wouldn't be able to use it. I did get a pamphlet about how to volunteer my time, should I ever get into a position where I could afford to do so.

I was sitting on a bench at the bus stop when I remembered the bartender wanting me to return and talk more about the coin around my neck. The night before, I had been almost certain I would never go back. In the light of day, with no other prospects, I couldn't think of a reason not to. Maybe he'd even give me another free beer.

As soon as a bus headed downtown pulled in, I jumped on it. I was getting comfortable, my backpack on the empty seat beside me, when I happened to glance back and saw spiky brown hair a few rows back. I knew I was staring, but I was in such shock that I couldn't help myself. How had Beak Nose gotten on the same bus I was going to take, when I didn't even realize I would be on it until a few minutes before it pulled in?

"Don't be paranoid, Jack," I muttered. Yeah, I talk to myself. It's been a habit since I was a kid. Usually I did it to process thoughts that my brain was having trouble with, or when working through a particularly hefty problem. I'm not too prideful to admit that this time it was from fear. Seeing the guy on my first bus of the morning could have been coincidence. After all, he was dressed in an old army-green jacket that looked like it was thirty years old, and his messy hair and stubble suggested someone who lived rough. Maybe he rode buses as a way to get off the streets during the day, or for a place to sleep.

I'd never seen him even dozing, though. He was always alert and wide eyed. And glancing in my direction as I stared at him. There was nothing in his eyes to say he was watching me, but I could tell his attention was focused in my direction even when he wasn't looking.

As soon as the bus reached the first stop near downtown, I bolted off. By chance, my bank had a branch a block away. I hustled over as quickly as I could without running, and then stopped inside to stare through the glass walls as the bus drove by. Beak Nose was still on it, staring at me as he passed, his eyes meeting mine for a second.

Now I was convinced something was going on. As nonchalant and unconcerned as he appeared when I was on the bus, his gaze had just been very piercing. The expression on his face spoke of rage and hatred. And it seemed to be directed at me.

The security guard was staring at me, and I suddenly realized how suspicious I must look. A guy running into the building just to stand by the window and stare out, carrying a backpack that looked to be stuffed with every worldly possession. Because it was.

I gave him a sickly smile and turned to approach the counter with deposit slips. I filled one out, and then waited in a short line to deposit my check. The teller printed out a balance receipt, which made me grin. It was the first time I'd seen triple digits in my account in too long, even if it was the very low triple digits.

Back on the street, I looked around to make sure Beak Nose hadn't gotten off the bus and circled back. Sighing with relief when I didn't see him, I headed for the nearest entrance to the Riverwalk. It was late enough that the morning rush was dying down, and early enough that tourists were still in bed. The sidewalks were lightly populated, and I didn't have to worry about bumping into anyone as I got lost in thought while walking.

Everything had started with the package from Jen. Well, I guess it all actually started when Jen left our home and went off to start working for some mysterious friends. It just took a few months to catch up to me. If I really was being followed by Beak Nose, then he had to be after the coin. My hand reached up to touch it, reassuring myself it was still around my neck. The question was, were they after the coin because it was gold and silver and probably worth a good bit, or were they after it because it supposedly had magical powers?

I stopped to get a couple of breakfast tacos from a hole in the wall Mexican restaurant, spending a few of my hard-earned dollars. They were still warm when I pulled open the door and entered Lyon's Den. I'd been expecting to find the door locked, but I'd come to learn later that it never was. Richard was behind the bar, almost in the same spot he'd been in when I left the day before. He looked up and smiled. "I wasn't sure I'd see you again, Jack Dahlish."

"I wasn't sure I'd come back," I admitted. As I approached the bar, I held up the bag. "I got some breakfast tacos, if you're hungry."

Richard leaned back in surprise, breaking into a grin. "Now, if that isn't a sign of fate then I don't know what is. Jennifer always brought food from that same place when she'd visit in the morning."

"She visited that often?" I pulled four tacos from the bag. Two were bacon and egg, and two were bean and cheese. I grabbed one of each, opening the first and stuffing it into my mouth.

"Yes, she became quite the frequent flier in her last few weeks." His smile slipped at the thought that she'd never be around again. "She became obsessed with the Nox and was always pumping me for more information. Your sister could be quite tenacious when she wanted something."

I smiled, remembering more than a few instances that backed that up. "Yeah, Jen could never be denied when she decided she needed to know something. I saw her spend three days in a library once just to research everything discovered about the Earth's core, solely because of a movie we watched about some scientists having to go down there and start it spinning again."

Richard was chewing, staring over my head as he thought about my sister. "The more I think of it, I should have known what she was up to. At the end, I mean. She kept pestering me

169

with questions about Relics, where they come from, how to de-termine if something was one. And she'd slip in questions about the Nine every now and then, too. She must have had the coin in her possession and was trying to decide what to do with it."

"How would she get it, though? That's what I can't figure out."

"As I said yesterday, she was working as a courier for the Magpie. He or she must have trusted your sister a good deal to let her carry something like the Blood of the Gods around."

"Explain that name to me. I get why you call it 'one of the Nine' if there are nine of the coins. But why Blood of the Gods?"

"That is more what the Nox have named the talismans. You see, there's no one with the ability to tell Nox from human when they are wearing their human masks, a shapeshifting abil-ity that has evolved over the millennia. So when the Nine were discovered, granting the wearer the ability not just to see through the masks but detect where Nox have been and tell them apart, it created quite a bit of fear in their community. Since the Nox were born of the gods, they think that only some-one with the blood of those same gods could do such a thing. Hence the name."

"Huh, that makes it sound like they don't much like the people wearing the coins. Didn't you say they served as protec-tors for the Nox?"

Richard pursed his lips and shook his head. "In a way, yes. Mostly they ensure that the Nox and humanity don't go to war again. If a Nox steps out of line and attacks humans, then one of the Nine have to intervene. Same goes if a human discovers the Nox and tries to exterminate or expose them. Having the world find out about them again would be a very bad thing, Jack. Ask me about the Wojna one day when you have a few hours."

I had so many questions that my head was full with them, but I had to get back on track with the most important thing. "Then Jen was transporting the coin," I reached up to touch it, something I found myself doing more and more, "and someone killed her for it?"

"That's possible," Richard said. "Based on the questions she was asking me, though, I'd say it's more that she was questioning if she should even deliver the package. She asked a few times how someone would get in touch with one of the Nine if they needed help."

"What did you say? That's something I'd like to know, so this thing can go to someone who can use it properly."

Richard was shaking his head as I spoke. "The only one of the Nine I knew well was the last person to wear *that* coin. His name was Albert Placencia, and he was a good man."

"Okay, where is he? Why did he take this thing off in the first place?" I lifted the coin and let it drop against my chest.

"He's dead. It must be five years now. He went up against a vampire brood that gave in to the thirst for human blood, and he didn't take backup." His eyes were on the bar as he spoke, the white rag rubbing the same spot over and over. "It took

171

almost a year before we could clear the nest and recover his body. The talisman was nowhere to be found."

"Until my sister was handed a package with it inside. I'm surprised they don't keep their couriers from looking at whatever they're carrying."

"They do," Richard said. "Usually, the item will be locked in one of those metal briefcases, or perhaps inside a container truck if it's large. Couriers are told where to take it, never what's inside. Your sister, though, was too curious for her own good. My guess is that she overheard something that made her think the coin was inside. Anyone with even a peripheral knowledge of the Nox world has heard rumors about one of the Nine missing."

"That sounds like my sister." I suddenly realized I had started taking all of this seriously. I hadn't even blinked at the mention of vampires, or the idea of someone getting killed fighting them. Was this how insanity started, talking to one person and then beginning to think they made a kind of sense? "If we accept that she was supposed to be delivering the coin for the Magpie, how do I find that person?"

The bartender sighed heavily, balling up the trash from our late breakfast and tossing it in a trashcan behind the bar. "I can understand your need for answers, Jack, but do you really want to do this? Risk your own life just to find out who killed your sister?"

"It's not just about finding her killer. That person has to be brought to justice. It's the right thing to do, and if the cops can't be bothered then I'll take care of the job myself."

"Now you sound like one of the Nine," he said with a half-smile. "After you left last night, I asked a few people I trust to keep things to themselves. Billy Wish is known as someone you go to if you're in need. No one is sure exactly what he does, but some people have left his club carrying enough cash to ease their financial worries. Considering everything we know about your sister, that tells us he has to be one of the Magpie's agents."

"Or the Magpie himself," I said insistently. "I'm telling you, the kind of muscle he had in the back room of Shine was more than some mid-level person would rate."

"Careful with assumptions, Jack. No one knows how big the Magpie's organization is, but it wouldn't surprise me to learn it compares to some Fortune 500 corporations. The kind of money they toss around speaks of very deep pockets. Regardless, one of my regulars happened to know that Billy leaves the club every morning at sunrise. No matter the season, it's always right at sunrise."

"Strange. Where does he go?"

Richard shrugged. "Can't say on that, my informant didn't know and wasn't brave enough to follow even to satisfy a corvid's curiosity."

"Interesting. I wish I had known last night so I could have left work a bit early and tried to follow him. I should have stuck around instead of leaving."

"No, Jack. Trust me on this, you don't want to hang out in here until you're sure about how you plan to handle the coin. If you're not going to accept the role of one of the Nine, then you

173

don't want any of the Nox to know you have it. That will lead to nothing but trouble."

I was stroking the coin again through my shirt. Part of me was warming to the idea of keeping it, but I knew I'd need to know a lot more about these Nox and what they were before I decided. Apparently, vampires were real and one form of Nox. That made me start thinking about other mythological and folk-lore creatures, and I began to wonder how many supposedly ex-isted.

"You look tired, Jack. You just mentioned leaving work early, so I'm guessing you work at night like I do." He eyed me, looking down to where he could have seen my backpack without the solid wooden bar in the way. "Do you have a place to stay?"

My face flushed with embarrassment. Even after so many weeks, I still hated admitting to people that I was homeless. Without even thinking about doing it, I found myself spilling the story of my debts, lost job, and apartment eviction. What made it all worse was knowing it was partly my own fault for poking my nose into things that I couldn't handle. If not for the hospital stay and recuperation, I would have still been doing fine and living in my old apartment. Maybe even eating cookies with Mrs. Wisson, sharing stories about Jen.

"Well, there's no way I'm letting you walk out of here like that." Richard flung the white towel over his shoulder and waved for me to get up and follow him. "I live in the back. It's not much, but it's home and I like it. You can grab some sleep here, get a shower and a hot meal."

174

"You don't have to do that," I protested, feeling like I was intruding. "I'm sure I'll find a shelter with a bed for me."

"Nonsense! If you think it's taking advantage or something foolish like that, you can come back tomorrow and help out in the kitchen. I always have a ton of dirty glasses needing to be washed, and I believe in giving the job personal attention."

Soon after I got settled on Richard's bed, over my objections that the couch would be fine, I managed to fall asleep while listening to the noise of people entering the Den for the light lunch he served. I'd learned that he never served alcohol until after noon, but it sounded like a surprising number of people showed up for their first drink around then. Well, a surprising number of Nox. Wrapping my head around the changes in my view of the world was going to take some time.

I slept until almost five, when Richard woke me gently to suggest I grab a shower and then head out before the dinner crowd started to arrive en masse. There were only a few people in the bar as I walked out, and Richard stopped me just long enough to pass me a brown paper bag. "I made you a burger. Grass fed organic beef on a whole wheat bun."

"You've been too good to me," I said. "I'm practically a total stranger."

"I knew your sister, Jack, and a woman like that doesn't spring from a family that would produce a bad seed. Come back in the morning, if you'd like, and you can start paying me back."

I nodded my thanks and turned to leave. I saw the man Richard had called Terrance the previous evening, sitting on the same stool he'd occupied before. He was staring at me again, but his gaze was on my chest. I felt certain this time that he was staring at the coin, as if he could sense it. Richard seemed to notice, as he stepped over. "Another round, Terrance? Looks like it's going to be a busy night, so I might as well take care of you now."

With his attention diverted, I made a quick exit. The Riverwalk was packed with tourists, enjoying their Saturday evenings. I wished I could be as carefree and relaxed as they all seemed to be. I was ravenous after sleeping most of the afternoon away, and I pulled the burger from the bag to take a giant bite. It was probably one of the most delicious burgers I'd ever tasted, even with only mustard and lettuce added. The bag also contained a bag of baked chips and a Ziploc bag filled with apple slices. Whatever else he was, the bartender seemed to have a very healthy outlook on food.

I climbed to street level at the first stairs I encountered and took a look at the street to get my bearings. I wasn't overly familiar with downtown, but I knew enough to recognize where I was and how to get to the bus stop I always used. I had to go several blocks north and east, and it was starting to get late. I knew I had to hurry if I was going to make the bus and get to work on time, so I decided to cut through a long alley that bypassed a few blocks.

Traffic opened up at that moment, and I was able to jog across the street and head for the dim space between two tall office buildings. The alley was dark and very humid in the late June heat, but I was able to walk quickly while avoiding the crush of tourists. It gave me time to finish the burger, as well, which I was enjoying more and more with each bite.

When I tripped and almost fell, I thought at first that I'd hit a piece of cracked concrete that rose above the rest.

Then I heard a loud shriek close behind me and turned in terror to see two men detaching from the shadowy alley walls I'd just passed. They were both beak nosed, with weak chins leading to sloping necks, and had spiky brown hair and stubble. I looked from one to the other, unable to see any difference between them.

"Who are you?" I asked shakily. "What do you want?"

One of the men opened his mouth wide, and the shrieking cry filled the alley again. I winced and raised my hands to cover my ears, the burger and bag of food dropping to the ground. The sound made me think of hawks circling in the sky, or eagles swooping for prey.

As the echoes faded, the other spoke in a grating voice. "Give us the talisman, and you can leave. Give it now!" Without waiting for an answer, he pounced forward. His hands were raised, clenched like talons. His sharp nails looked brown and filthy.

In an instant, I realized I wasn't seeing human hands. The skin was hard and wrinkled, reminding me of a chicken's foot. Reddish brown feathers covered his wrists, disappearing beneath the cuff of the faded green army jacket. When I looked up at his face, I saw the nose and mouth had grown and become a short beak with a small pink tongue visible when he opened it and let out a short shriek. His face and head were covered in rusty brown feathers, with very human eyes glaring at me.

His twin had shifted into the same birdlike form, waiting a few steps back as if seeing how I would react. They both seemed to realize that I could see their true forms at the same time, squawking in surprise. I took the opportunity to turn and run, and then tripped again over the line of almost invisible string that had been run across the alleyway. My hands shot out to stop my fall, scraping on the rough concrete path.

There was chittering laughter behind me, and I turned my head to see the birdmen approaching. "Give us the coin!" one screeched, holding out a scaly hand.

I flipped over and landed on my butt, trying to crawl away from them. I could feel the coin growing heavier around my neck, and heat seemed to be building up on my chest. I raised my hand to pull it away from my skin, and then cried out in shock when my fingers were burned. The birdmen were getting closer, their beady eyes locked on my chest as their talons reached out, looking sharp enough to rip me apart.

The alley was suddenly filled with blinding white light, and I felt a searing pain on my chest as I raised my hands to shield my eyes. The birdmen shrieked in pain, and I heard a wild fluttering sound that faded down the alley. Within seconds, the light began to subside until I was able to lower my hands and blink as I tried to get the spots out of my vision. Once I could see again, I was alone in the alley. There was a large hole in my shit the size of a dinner plate, and the skin on my chest was red and raw.

I raised a hand to the coin experimentally, and found it cool to the touch now. That coolness seemed to pulsate through my skin, and I closed my eyes as I gasped at the feeling. When I looked again, the skin on my chest and fingers was no longer red and burned. It was as if the coin had healed the harm it caused while protecting me.

Grabbing my backpack from where it had fallen from my shoulder, I held it in front of my chest as I rushed out of the alley. I wasn't entirely sure what had just happened, but any lingering doubts about the existence of the Nox had just been extinguished.

NOW

I was careful to avoid moving too quickly as I circled around a few blocks to approach the building that had once housed Shine from the back. It was late enough that the streets were almost empty, but early enough that some cars did pass by now and then. I wanted to make sure I looked like nothing more than a normal person taking a stroll. Standing out in someone's memory could come back to haunt me if something went wrong.

And then something *did* go wrong. I was in an alley between two buildings, only twenty or so feet from the back of the warehouse, when I encountered an eight-foot-tall chain link fence. Some kind of green material had been woven through the links, preventing anyone from seeing what was on the other side. On top of the fence was a loosely coiled strand of barbed wire. I almost reached forward to see if I could climb the fence, before I noticed a small sign a few feet to my left that warned of electricity.

Whatever was going on in the supposedly vacant warehouse that had once been a hot club, the owners wanted it protected. I was baffled, considering the decrepit exterior that was visible from the street. Anyone looking at it would think the building was a few years from being torn down to make way for something newer and better. Definitely not worth the effort or expense this fence seemed to imply.

I wasted another ten minutes circling around to approach from another alley, one that would put me on the side of the club where I'd had my encounter with Billy Wish's goons ten years before. My memories of anything but the beating that night were hazy, but I could remember a black mouth that would indicate a smaller alley branching off the large one we'd been in that led to the main street at the front of the club.

There was a fence at the end of this alley, as well. It was just as tall, just as electrified, and just as frustrating. The only good thing to come of it was that there were no visible cameras, so I didn't have to worry about already being detected. I almost called Nyk to tell him we'd have to keep staking out the club to see who exited, but as I pulled out my phone, I glanced at the buildings to either side of me.

One was a storage building, painted orange and white with a large window on the second level showing a row of doors that I doubted led anywhere. The other was a warehouse for a feed store company, and based on the smell it probably contained thousands of bags of chicken feed or deer corn. It was a smell I'd grown familiar with during summer weeks spent in the country with relatives growing up.

That second building also had a rusty ladder leading up to the roof. It was eight feet off the ground, but close enough to an old dumpster that I felt sure I could make a jump to grab the first rung and pull myself up.

I did exactly that, after falling on my ass the first time and jarring every bone in my body. Wounded pride drove me to try again, and my hand caught the rung that time. My sweaty palm almost made me slip off, but I managed to get a grip with my other hand and then started pulling myself up.

"Gym," I whispered through heavy breaths. "Gotta start going to the gym." My arms were burning after three pulls, and by the time I was able to get my feet on the first rung and take my weight off them, my shoulders were aching like I'd been stretched out on a Medieval rack device.

Once I made it onto the roof of the feed warehouse, I was a few feet above the roofline of Shine. That vantage point allowed me to see an array of large HVAC systems, with ducting running between many of them. Almost hidden behind those large metal forms was a cluster of antennas and satellite dishes. All of them looked nearly new, highlighted by the moonlight that shone on them through cracks in the cloudy sky.

That was a lot of expensive hardware for a building that was supposed to be vacant and unused the last five years. I felt even better about my idea that the Magpie was inside. A surge of gleeful excitement filled me at the thought that I had found the villain's secret lair. I almost did a little dance, but sanity reasserted itself before I got that out of hand.

I stared over at Shine for several seconds, gathering myself and then reaching up to touch the coin under my shirt. With a deep breath, I opened my senses and turned my enhanced vision on the club. I could see streaks of Nox essence all over the roof, a dull yellow that I'd long identified as belonging to creatures like ogres and trolls alongside a fainter silver that almost shimmered in the night. That essence I wasn't familiar with, though it was similar to some others I'd detected in the past. I wished

I were closer, so I could get a sense of the taste and smell of the essence. I need all three senses to really narrow things down.

The gap between the buildings was enormous from my perspective. It was ten feet, at least. Way more than I'd be comfortable trying to jump, even if I weren't more than twenty feet off the ground. I looked at other buildings nearby, finding one at the rear of the club that had a gap of only four or five feet. I couldn't find a way to get onto that building, however.

Checking my phone, I saw I was coming up fast on the thirty minute timeline I'd given Nyk. I thought about calling, but figured I could get back to the ground and see if maybe the other building had some way to get onto the roof. If so, I could risk that jump to get onto Shine and find a way inside.

My shoulders started yelling at me the minute I started climbing down the ladder again, and they hated it even more when I hung from the bottom rung for a few seconds before dropping to the concrete. Luckily, I was so cold that my shivering kept me from thinking about my shoulders too much. My hands were like blocks of ice after the climb up and down on the bare metal rungs, and the wind on top of the feed warehouse had been colder than expected. For a second, I wished I had worn my coat, expensive or no.

The building directly behind Shine turned out to be an old brick building from the 1920s or '30s. The street level had once been a television repair place, and there was still fading white letters on the windows advertising their services. Those windows were dusty and almost opaque, speaking of years of vacancy. There was a second floor above, with small windows

183

facing the street. Both sides of the building were solid brick, and I almost yelled with joy when I found another ladder.

That joy was quickly snuffed when I realized the first rung was just as high up as the other ladder I'd climbed, and this time there was no handy dumpster nearby to climb on. I wasted a few minutes searching and then carrying over a few small wooden crates that felt like they'd fall apart if I set them down too hard. With my six-foot height, I felt sure I'd only need a boost of a few feet before I could jump and catch the first rung.

I didn't fall this time, catching the rung on my first try. The crates had broken into several pieces as I jumped, so I never would have had a second attempt. I could barely feel my fingers by the time I was on the roof of the building, cursing myself for never wearing gloves even when nights were going to be close to freezing. I tucked my hands under my armpits, trying to warm them as I walked to the edge of the roof and looked across the gap between this building and Shine.

The space seemed wider than it had when I saw it from the feed warehouse, but not by much. I tried to pump myself up, thinking about running track in my high school years. I'd tried out for the long jump team but been in the lower half of the results and didn't make the team. My best jump back then had been around thirteen feet. Surely, I could manage half that even as a man twenty years older.

I decided not to give myself time to overthink it, taking a dozen steps back and then running forward. I could feel my body wanting me to stop before I reached the edge, pleading with me to not do this stupid thing. But I kept going, planting my food on the short ledge around the roof and pushing myself up and forward.

My shin banged against the sharp edge of Shine's roof, and I cried out as I fell face first onto the loose gravel that covered it. Groaning, I rolled over onto my back, and raised a hand to my nose and lip to make sure they weren't bleeding. I breathed a sigh of relief, but I could tell from the way my face was throbbing I'd wake up to bruises the next day. My shin was another story, and I could already feel the trickle of blood from where it had impacted the building. I was able to put my weight on it with no problem, though, so I pushed it from my mind and took a look around.

There had to be a way onto this roof from inside the building, since I'd seen no ladders on the walls of the building itself. There was no possible place for a doorway, so I looked around for some kind of trapdoor. I didn't have to look for long, finding one only a few feet from the edge of the back corner. The metal door was painted white, probably to keep from absorbing too much of the summer heat, and it stood out in the midst of the gray gravel.

I hurried over and tugged on the twisted rebar handle of the door. Fully expecting it to give no more than an inch before proving locked, I was surprised when it opened with ease. There was a quiet squeal from the hinges, but not loud enough to make me fear it had been heard from within. Once the trap door opened, I was able to see a short ladder leading down to a metal catwalk. With only a second's hesitation, I threw caution

to the wind and quickly descended, pulling the door closed quietly above me.

On the catwalk, I could see that I was far above the floor of
the warehouse. It looked nothing like it had during my three
nights searching Shine for Billy or my sister. In fact, it looked
like someone had cleared everything of value at some point and
left behind only broken things that were worthless. Ninety percent of the floor below me was exposed, covered in open ship-
ping crates or scratched chairs. A small part of the back corner
opposite me had been walled off, and my memory was certain
that was the area I'd been escorted to, the office with Billy Wish
and his bodyguards.

I could hear faint voices, and I moved as silently as possible
along the catwalks until I found myself above what looked to
be a clandestine meeting. The lawyer, Chatterton, was perched
delicately on the edge of a chair. Five others sat with him, forming a rough circle with an open space between them. Two were
the concealed figures Nyk and I had observed approaching and
entering the building, still hidden within the hoods. They sat
close together, obviously a cohesive unit.

One man looked like he belonged in a Miami mobster film,
and I recognized him as Harold Goldblatt. He'd traded the yellow Hawaiian shirt for a white button up over khaki trousers,
but still wore the straw hat and had another fat cigar smoking in
his mouth. He looked completely at ease among the others, and
I wondered if he had expected me to be here when he left the
card for us to find at his house.

The fourth was a real shock, a face I was familiar with, being a San Antonio native. He was a big property developer and owned a string of other businesses across town. His face had been on billboards and television commercials since my childhood. The man had to be in his eighties by now, and I never would have pegged him for being involved in the Nox black market.

The last person was dressed in a dark suit, with a black tie over an almost blindingly white shirt. She was short, maybe a few inches over five feet, with her black hair cut into a neck length fringe. I felt my stomach knot up as I recognized her. She'd been one of Billy's bodyguards, the one who spoke to me in the alley and did most of the damage before everyone else piled on.

I opened my senses, looking at each member of the group. The air was filled with Nox trails of all size and color, obscuring any kind of identifiers around the people below me. The catwalk was wild with essence, as well, and I was overwhelmed with the smell of earthy body odor and rotting meat. *Definitely ogres and trolls*, I thought. They must serve as security for the Magpie or whichever of his agents still used the empty building. It was so overwhelming that I had to close myself off after a few seconds, returning to my human senses.

"We can't keep operating as normal with one of the Nine onto us," Chatterton was saying. "This is a time for caution. We need to sell some assets and move our operations to another city. Temporarily," he emphasized as some of the others stiffened.

187

"You know *I'm* not going anywhere," Goldie said, holding his lit cigar between two fingers and pointing it at the lawyer. "My stores have given me a very respectable face in this city, and no one has ever suspected my involvement with this operation." He laughed, a loud guffawing that surprised me. "It's not like the people here could figure out what we're up to even if they did suspect me. It's all drugs or money laundering to their minds, and they can't even grasp the kinds of things we deal with."

"We've all made fortunes here," the property developer said, his bass voice conjuring memories of all the times I'd seen him on TV, spouting his inane catch phrase. "We can't put that at stake by continuing to operate under the nose of the one person who could slow us down. I've been thinking of retiring for a while, and this is the perfect time." He stood up, rubbing his hand down his pants to brush off any dust from the old chair he'd been sitting on. "Consider this my resignation from the Circle. I'll take offers for buying my shares anytime you want to reach out." With that, he turned and strode from the room. The others watched him leave in silence, until we all heard the sound of the door thudding closed behind him.

"We are new to this," said one of the hooded figures, a female voice with an intriguing European accent.

"My sister and I will stay, but we agree to moving operations." The other hooded figure was a man, his accent a mirror of the woman's.

"The carrier of the talisman is unknown to us," the hooded woman said, "but we have dealt with members of the Nine before. They should not be underestimated." Her brother nodded in agreement.

"I know Dahlish," the suited woman said, her voice sending chills through me as I remembered the last time I'd heard it. "He's always been a fool. A crusader, always set on doing the right thing and blind to anything else around him until that's done. Give me two weeks, a month at the most, and I'll have him so distracted he wouldn't notice if we were operating right under his nose."

"I met him today," Goldie said, drawing the stares of the others. "He and the bounty hunter came to my house. They tracked me down through all the corporate records for those shell corporations you keep creating, Cissie. Anyone who digs that deeply isn't going to go away until he's satisfied that he's found what he's looking for. We all know what that is."

"Why?" the hooded female asked. "Why is he so obsessed in this search?"

"Because of his sister," the suited woman, apparently Cissie, said. "She was one of our couriers years ago, and the idiot girl let her curiosity overrule her common sense."

Both hooded figures hissed. "This is not good," the male said. "People will go to great lengths to get revenge if you touch their family."

"It's not a big deal," Cissie said sternly, staring hard at each of the others. "As far as he's concerned, he got his revenge ten years ago. My feeling is that Walsh brought him in on this, and if we can find whoever hired the bounty hunter, then we can put an end to it."

"I did," Goldie said triumphantly, grinning widely around the cigar clamped in his teeth.

"What did you say?" Cissie asked slowly, her words colder than the north pole.

"I'm the one who hired Nyk Walsh and tasked him with finding the Magpie. Through an intermediary, of course."

"Why the hell would you do something so stupid?"

"Because I wanted to see just how secure you were in your position," Goldie said, leaning forward with anticipation. "If there's any weakness in the Circle, we need to know so we can cut it out."

The others were staring at him in horror, the hooded siblings hissing even louder. Cissie rose to her feet and started to advance on the grinning man, cracking the knuckles on each fist. I felt sure violence was about to happen, and I wasn't sure if I should try to intervene.

At that moment, my phone began buzzing loudly in my pocket. I fumbled quickly with my frozen fingers to pull it from my jeans and silence the vibrating buzz. The screen showed that Nyk was calling, and I realized I'd been gone for far more than the thirty minutes agreed upon. I pressed a button to darken the screen again, and then looked up to see how Goldie was faring.

Five pairs of eyes met mine, two of them almost glowing within the dark confines of their hoods. I felt my heart racing, trying to think of what to do. "Um. Hi," I said lamely.

THEN

I sat huddled on my seat, my backpack held tightly against my chest. Buildings and cars passed outside the bus as I stared with unseeing eyes, lost in replaying the memory of what had happened in the alley. What had those things been, men who had feathers and faces like birds? Where had the bright light and heat come from that poured out of the coin to frighten them away?

There was still a large hole in my shirt, proof that it had all happened and wasn't a figment of my imagination. If not for that, I'd be convinced I'd gone as crazy as I'd assumed the homeless woman and bartender to be. I still wasn't completely sure it hadn't happened, and more than once I almost stalked the aisle of the bus to ask the other passengers if they could see the ragged hole over my chest.

My phone began to ring, an annoying pop song that I'd downloaded and used to make sure I always heard it. It was sheer automatic movement that made me grab it from my pocket and press the button to answer the call. "Hello," I said numbly.

"You just had to open the package, didn't you, Jack?" The voice was familiar, and it only took a few seconds to recognize Billy's mocking tone. "Too convinced that your precious sister would never put you in harm's way, perhaps? Well, she did, buddy. Big time."

"I thought you didn't know Jen," I said through gritted teeth.

"I've been reminded," he said. "One of our couriers. We pay them to transport items, not look at them. We pay them quite well for that."

"You sent those things after me," I said with sudden realization. "What the hell are they?"

He laughed, a cackling sound that made me wince. "Those were a couple of tengu, pal. A pair of Nox that are sick and tired of humanity stepping on them and holding them down. I promised them a fortune if they got the coin back for me, Jack. How did you do it? I've never seen anyone draw on the power of the Nine so soon after putting it on."

"Why don't you come meet me, and I'll show you."

Billy laughed again, genuine amusement this time. "I really would enjoy that, Jacky boy. More than you can imagine. Tell you what, if you think you're so tough all of a sudden, meet me where your last saw your sister. One hour, Jack." The phone went dead, and I put it back in my pocket with a shaking hand.

When the bus stopped outside of the building I worked in, I stayed in my seat. I knew I was putting my newfound financial stability in jeopardy, but I had something more important to do. My fingers were clenched on my backpack, so hard that I could feel them aching. I thought briefly about going to get a gun. The process would take an hour or two, however, and I didn't have time for that. For the first time in my life, I truly wished I knew the sorts of people who could just open a car trunk and sell me a weapon.

Two stops later, I got off the bus and began an impatient wait. I'd been travelling in the opposite direction of where I needed to go, and it took almost ten minutes for a bus heading that way to stop. I clambered onto it, taking a seat in the very back. Once the bus was in motion, I unzipped the main compartment of my backpack and pulled out a clean shirt. I changed quickly, drawing a few curious looks when people noticed the hole in front of my old shirt. That question was answered.

Twilight was beginning to descend by the time I left the bus in the quiet neighborhood. I could hear the sounds of kids playing somewhere and imagined them sprinting around in a backyard. A few sprinklers were running, adding a repeated shush-shush-shush sound to the air. I stared at the entrance to the gravel path for a minute, breathing deeply and asking myself if I really wanted to do this.

Finally, I decided that I *had* to do it. It didn't matter how much want was involved. I grasped the coin through my shirt and took slow steps until my feet were crunching on loose gravel. The road was no more than a hundred feet, widening out to a small parking area once it was behind the two houses it passed between. I could see one vehicle there, a black SUV that looked large enough to carry a football team.

A man in a black suit waited beside the SUV, smoking and watching my approach through mirrored sunglasses. He didn't move except to raise the cigarette to his lips every few seconds for a quick pull, until I was a few steps away. Then he slowly moved his head to indicate that I should keep walking, toward the jogging path.

Two more suited guards waited there, one of them the small woman. She smirked at me, then held out a hand. I stared at it, confused, until I realized she wanted my backpack. I passed it over, expecting her to search it for weapons. She only tossed it to the ground while her partner made me raise my arms and then patted me down thoroughly. Too thoroughly. Even if I'd managed to find a gun, I never would have made it anywhere near Billy with it.

"Want me to turn my head and cough?" I asked the goon when he was a little too thorough.

"Just had to make sure you weren't a total moron," the woman said, still smirking. "I mean, you have to be pretty stupid to come back for more after last time, but I guess we can mark some of that down as bravery. Are you brave, Mr. Dahlish?"

"Not particularly," I muttered.

She laughed, reaching out to nudge the mountain of a man beside her. "What do you know, Tol? The kid's got a few brain cells rattling around in there, after all." She turned and started walking along the jogging path, and the man with her held out his hand for me to follow before he took up position behind me.

I could see a mop of brownish blonde hair on top of a slim figure standing on the small bridge over the drainage ditch, leaning against the handrail. Billy Wish was dressed in a wife-beater and torn blue jeans that probably cost more than the paycheck I'd received that morning. His arms showed a bit of

194

gristly muscle but were almost stick thin. He turned at the sound of steps on the wooden bridge.

The female bodyguard took up position to the side and just behind him, holding her arms crossed at the wrist in front of her stomach. The large man behind me put a hand on my shoulder as I stepped onto the bridge, holding me in that spot. His presence was overwhelming, and I started to wonder just why I'd fallen for this little meeting that was an obvious trap.

"Jacky boy showed up," Billy said in mocking tones. "I didn't think you'd have the balls." He pulled a hundred-dollar bill from his pocket, passing it to the woman who took it with a grin. "Now you just cost me a Benjamin, and you're wearing something stolen from me. Not off to a good start, are you?"

I knew I should feel fear, and I did. Mostly, though, I felt a growing sense of sad resignation. Whatever happened on this bridge, it would be the end of my desperate search for answers. I looked over at the tall grass, the place my sister had been dumped.

"When she was seven, she asked me to show her how to ride a bike."

"Huh?" Billy asked, looking around as if someone else might know what I was talking about.

"Can you imagine being that old, all your friends riding around the neighborhood, and you can't join them? Jen asked me to teach her, but I was too busy playing video games with my friends. No twelve-year-old boy would rather spend time with his bratty little sister." I smiled at the memory, something I'd not thought about in years.

"What are you talking about, buddy?" Billy leaned his head forward, squinting at me. "Are you loco, or something?"

"When she was ten, she asked me if I'd show her how to dance. Her school was having a Sadie Hawkins, she wanted to ask a boy to go with her but was afraid to do it until she knew she could dance with him." I shook my head and laughed, looking up at the deepening purple sky. "But a friend of mine had just gotten his license, and he was going to let me drive on some dirt roads outside the city. So I told her no."

Billy turned to the woman, her smile fading. "What the fuck is wrong with him? Did you hit his head too hard or something last time?"

"After she turned twelve, Jen wanted me to drive her to Austin for a movie with some of her friends. My parents were working, and I had nothing else to do. I was sitting around playing Nintendo, killing time. I said no, because I didn't want to spend an afternoon with a bunch of little girls." I reached up to wipe away a tear, trying to hold back the flood behind it.

"Dude, is he on drugs or something?" Billy was leaning around me to talk to the large man still holding my shoulder. I felt that hand move slightly, and knew he'd shrugged.

"Before she turned sixteen, she begged me to show her how to drive. All I needed to do was spend a few hours with her over a couple of weekends, let her get used to being behind the wheel. I was twenty-one, though, and enjoying my new ability to hit bars and clubs with my friends. I promised we'd do it next weekend, and then I promised to do it the weekend after that, and the weekend after that." I kept my gaze on the tall grass where the body had been discovered.

"Okay, why didn't someone tell me this guy is cuckoo for cocoa puffs? I'm wasting my time out here."

"When she was nineteen, Jen asked me to listen while she talked about something important. Ten minutes of my time, that's all she needed. But I was too busy, and I couldn't stop that long. I had to get dressed and go out for a drink with friends." I shook my head, laughing at my stupidity as I turned to him. "Ten minutes, Billy. Can you imagine not making ten minutes for your own sister?"

Billy held his fingers in front of my face, snapping them a few times. "Hey, buddy. No one here cares about your little family dramas. That's not what we're here for."

"But it is," I told him. "When she was nineteen, my sister was murdered. Not because she was a bad person, but because she trusted the wrong people. By the time she realized that, and tried to do something about it, it was too late for her. It was too late for me. And it was definitely too late for you.

"We're here because I was too much of a selfish ass to give my sister a little of my time, and because you're too much of a selfish ass to consider how using these people touches on other lives." I waved my hand toward the spot where crime scene techs and officers had been combing the grass only days before, searching for any clue to find my sister's killer. To find the man standing in front of me now. I was sure of that. "You just killed her and dumped her body here. I don't know why you chose this spot, and frankly I don't care. But you need to realize that there are consequences."

"Consequences?" Billy cackled, slapping a hand to his stomach in exaggerated amusement. The woman standing behind him was no longer smirking, though. There was a look of intense concentration on her face now, and her eyes seemed to be locked on mine through her dark sunglasses. "There's no consequences here, bud. I'm Billy Wish, and I tell the world how it's going to be. You don't come here and tell me." He waved a hand over his shoulder. "Put a bullet in this wacko's head so we can get the coin and get out of here. This place smells too much like nature."

The woman stood there in silence for a few moments, but finally I saw her hand twitch and then move toward the gun holstered under her left arm. I saw it, but I didn't pay attention to it. I was focusing all my willpower on the coin hanging around my neck, trying to call forth the light and heat it had produced only a few hours earlier.

On the trip to the meeting, I had been trying to figure out what caused the coin to react. Richard had told me the coin gave the ability to detect Nox, see through their human disguises and follow the trails they left behind. That made a kind of sense to me, though it would prove to be vastly different to the reality I'd come to learn in later weeks. Nothing he had talked about pointed to the coin being a weapon, as it had seemed in that alley.

I decided that the coin must have acted to protect me. I figured that there must be a built-in desire to shield whoever

198

wore one of the coins, to keep them safe while they worked to maintain the balance between human and Nox. And I had decided that there was only one way I could hurt the man who'd killed my sister, even if it meant I had to let him hurt me, too.

"Too afraid to do it yourself, Billy?" I said the words quietly, almost whispering them in the still air. Frogs were croaking around the shores of the pond, and birds were singing their songs to the setting sun. The muffled roar of traffic from the nearby road hummed over it all. But Billy heard me. His bodyguards heard me, too. The woman's hand froze halfway to her weapon, and I felt the large paw on my shoulder tense.

Billy Wish turned confused wide eyes on me. "What the fuck did you just say to me?"

"I asked if you're too much of a chickenshit to pull the trigger yourself." I raised my eyes to meet his, hoping they conveyed the resolute determination I felt in that moment. "As you said, I had the balls to come out here and meet you. The least you can do is have the balls to do the dirty work yourself. Or do you need to borrow some from her?" I asked, raising my chin at the woman behind him.

Her smirk reappeared, and I could tell that she knew the kind of person she worked for. "Shoot him already!" Billy screamed, turning to look at her. She tilted her head as she examined me, and then swiftly pulled her gun. I braced for the shot, but instead she flipped it in her hand and held it out to him.

"You do it. Sir." The last word was dripping with scorn, and I saw his eyes go wide with shock.

"Come on, Mr. Magpie," I said, making my voice as mocking as his had been. "I'm just a loser, right? Just a poor ignorant human standing here surrounded by your goons. All you have to do is take the gun, point, and shoot." He was staring at the weapon, and I could see his lower lip quivering. If I'd thought about it, I would have sworn he was about to break down and cry. "But you can't do it, can you? So what does that make you?"

With a cry of rage, he grabbed the weapon. He fumbled it in his fingers before he got a good hold on the butt of the pistol, swinging it toward me. Suddenly, I found myself staring into the black hole of the barrel, licking my lips and regretting my plan to goad him into this very thing. "Come on," I said under my breath. "Come on." I begged the coin to act, to produce the light and heat again. It would startle Billy Wish enough to make him release the gun, and then I could grab it and shoot him before his bodyguards turned on me.

Nothing happened. The coin didn't begin to feel hot. There was no light growing in the encroaching darkness of evening. Absolutely nothing. I felt betrayed by everything I'd begun to believe.

Billy held the gun, snarling at me. Seconds passed, the number growing in the stillness of the pond. The woman didn't move, and the giant of a man standing over my shoulder was totally still. A low moan started, and for a while I thought it was coming from my own mouth as I felt my death approaching. But then I saw the gun begin to shake.

The moan grew louder, until Billy lowered the arm holding the gun until it was hanging from a few fingers by his thigh. I was stunned to still be alive, and looked to the woman to see that her smirk had turned into a grimace. "You really don't have the balls, do you?" she asked.

"That's what you're here for," Billy pouted. He had deflated, his shoulders slumped and his eyes on the boards between our feet. I almost felt bad for the little shit, except that he'd killed my sister.

It wasn't the way I'd planned things, but seeing the gun hanging there in his loose grip made me think I could still do what I'd come for. I tensed my legs, raising up on the balls of my feet. The hand on my shoulder was loose, almost as if the brute behind me had forgotten I was there. It would take no more than a handful of seconds to jump forward, grab the gun, and raise it. I just hoped I had the guts Billy didn't, to pull the trigger.

I was leaning forward to make my move when the woman bent to grab the gun. I almost cried out in frustration, seeing my chance snatched away because I hadn't acted quickly enough. She raised the weapon, and I waited for her to point it at me and pull the trigger as her boss had been unable to do.

The gun barked, a spray of bright light appearing as the bullet was ejected from the barrel at immense speed. Time seemed to almost stand still, and I felt like I was watching the bullet lazily fly through the air. It hit flesh with a wet smacking sound, sending bits of bone into the air with a spray of red blood.

Billy Wish collapsed on the bridge.

I saw surprise and shock, the last expressions on a dying face. His blood and brains were all over me, and I could feel the mess dripping from my chin as I stood looking down at him in stunned disbelief. The woman grunted, reached out a foot to delicately shove the body and make sure he was dead, and then holstered her weapon.

"Come on, Tol. We need to be gone when some citizen calls the cops about a gunshot." The heavy hand left my shoulder, a weight I'd become so accustomed to that I felt as if I'd float away for a moment. I couldn't pull my eyes from the corpse at my feet, or the growing red pool of blood that was dripping between the gaps in the wood planking of the bridge.

As she passed, the woman grabbed my chin in a steel grip and turned my face toward hers. "You'll get out of here, too, if you know what's good for you." She glanced away just long enough to look at Billy Wish and make a disgusted noise. "He should have known better than to try and take one of the Nine for himself. Damned idiot kid."

She released her grip on my chin, and I heard footsteps on the graveled jogging path as the two bodyguards calmly walked toward their SUV. I knew I needed to leave, too, but I couldn't seem to force my feet to move. I was spattered with blood and gore and standing over a dead body. There was no gun to suggest I shot him, but I knew that wouldn't present much of a problem to cops gifted with a tidy little case to quickly wrap up.

I heard the SUV's engine fire up, and then the sound of tires on gravel as it backed along the path to the road that would take them out of the subdivision. I couldn't make myself move, until I felt a hand take mine and pull me violently away. I looked around wildly, but there was no one there. Now that I was moving, though, it was easier to keep going. I grabbed my backpack as I passed it, still laying on the ground where the woman had dropped it, and started to jog down the path between the two houses.

There was a flare of light, as someone turned on a flashlight on the street ahead. The light bounced as they walked toward me, but they were only using it to guide their steps. Before they could raise the light and spot me, I darted off the path and along the fence at the back of the houses. The growth of trees and brush got heavier the farther I went from the small pond and jogging path, and I was able to duck down and hide there as several people walked into the parking area. Voices called out, asking if someone was hurt, and the flashlight was joined by others as people began to search around for the source of the noise they'd heard.

My shock from the moment on the bridge was wearing off, replaced by a growing exultation. Billy Wish, the man known as the Magpie, the man who'd ordered my sister's murder, was dead. It hadn't happened at my hand as I'd wanted, but it had happened because of my words. I had no doubts that the woman wouldn't have acted as she did if I hadn't goaded Billy into showing his weakness.

And maybe the stories of my sister had helped, too. Maybe Jen had gotten her own revenge in a way, working on the woman's emotions and causing her to see Billy for the bastard that he was.

Then I remembered the hand that had pulled me away from the body. A hand that saved me, since I would have been discovered standing over it by the people from nearby houses who even now cried out in shock and surprise as they discovered the dead man on the small bridge. Had that been Jen? A last act from beyond the grave? I didn't believe in ghosts, but if there were birdmen such as the tengu and apparently other fantastical creatures, then why not ghosts.

"Thank you, little sister," I said quietly to the darkness. "He's gone. You can rest now."

NOW

The woman I now knew as Cissie was the first to move. She screamed at the others to cover the exits, and then ran for a ladder I hadn't noticed before which led up to the catwalks. I still had my phone in my hand, so I frantically pulled up the call log and stabbed Nyk's name. My hand was so slick with nervous sweat that I felt it slipping. My brain was screaming that it was falling, but my body was so amped up and focused on external threats that I moved too slowly.

I watched the prepaid phone fall fifteen feet to the concrete below, where it smashed into a couple of pieces. My hopes for rescue were smashed along with it. The sound of footsteps on steel rungs told me Cissie was climbing fast and would be on the catwalk in seconds. I looked around for any other way down and out of the building, but there was nothing.

The trapdoor to the roof was my only option, so I turned and started running along the meshed metal to where I'd entered the building. I could retrace my steps, and if I was lucky, I'd make it back to Nyk's truck before anyone could call in goons to help them keep me contained. I was almost grinning in triumph as I thought about it. I knew who four of the people that had been meeting below me were. The two hooded figures were a mystery, but the others I could work to expose. With a little digging, I was positive I could uncover all kinds of illegal acts that would put them behind bars for years.

I reached the short ladder up to the trapdoor and leapt up to take the few rungs to the top. I pushed on the door, feeling it begin to swing open. A fresh cool breeze of night air surrounded me, feeding my happiness at escaping. For a brief second, I lamented that my fingers had just began to warm enough that I could feel them again.

Then a heavy weight descended on the trapdoor, and it smashed down. I'd been pushing my body up to make a quick exit, so the metal smashed against the top of my head with a sharp crack. The next thing I knew, I was laying on the catwalk under the trapdoor, staring up at the place I'd been seconds before. I could feel a tickle in my hair and knew there'd be a gash on top of my head when I raised my fingers to it.

"I had a feeling I should have put Tol on the roof tonight, but I thought there was no way anyone would find us here." From my perspective, it almost looked like she was hanging by her feet over a floor a short distance below. Then my brain caught up to my eyes, and I realized I was looking at her upside down.

Cissie was only ten feet away, leaning back against the railing of the catwalk. I groaned as I rolled over, and immediately felt blood trickle down my forehead. "You killed my sister," I said. "It wasn't Billy at all."

She shrugged but didn't admit it. "Your sister killed herself when she opened a package she was paid to transport. Does it really matter who pulled the trigger to complete the process?"

Things were starting to line up in my head. Things I should have realized much earlier, and it had taken a hard knock to jumble my brains enough to get through preconception. "You're the Magpie."

She smirked, reminding me of that long-ago night on a wooden bridge, and bowed slightly in acknowledgement. "Someone had to take the title, and I figured why not me. If Billy Wish could lead a group as powerful as the Circle, there was no reason that I couldn't do it. Hell, I could do it better."

"No." I pushed myself up to lean back against the railing, hoping I could sit long enough for the ringing in my head to subside. "Billy didn't have what it took, he couldn't even look me in the eyes when he was holding a gun in my face. That kid was never more than a figurehead."

"Look who's gone and grown a few more brain cells since the last time I saw him." Her smirk was still there, but it looked more wary now. "Billy really did think he was the Magpie. The little shit would swan around telling everyone how important he was, and you don't want to know how many of his little one-night stands ended with Tol and me dumping a body because he blabbed too much."

"But you were always there, the voice of reason when he tried to get too flamboyant or too reckless."

"Of course." She snorted, shaking her head with a laugh. "At first it was kind of refreshing, knowing I could wield so much power through him. He never even thought that he was being steered in certain directions. I let the kid make a few stupid moves, when I knew it wouldn't hurt the business too much. It also made him value my advice more."

"What business is that?" I asked, turning my head to look out over the empty warehouse. A flare of light and pain flashed through my head with the movement. "Stealing clubs from drunk goblins? Forcing a brownie to steal something for you so he can pay his debts?"

Cissie laughed louder, and behind it I heard the ringing sounds of someone else climbing the ladder to the catwalk. "Shit, Dahlish, you haven't figured that out yet? Ten years with one of the Nine, and you're still thinking like an unenlightened human. It's such a shame."

She pushed off from the railing, taking two quick steps and then squatting to grin at me. "I didn't make the brownie steal anything. What I bought from him was the most valuable thing he had. His memories. For three days, little Skel lived like a debauched king. He was in Shine every night, taking a new girl to his hotel suite afterward. And then he sold those memories to me, and the moment he signed the contract they were no longer his. I've made a lot of money these last few years selling that glimpse of Nox life to other people." A crashing sound came from below, and for a moment I thought I felt a cold draft.

"As for the goblin, Chip, he practically begged me to take his wealth away. We spent three hours finishing off a bottle of top shelf vodka down there," she looked toward the place I re-membered the bar being when I'd spent time in Shine. "All he did was piss and moan about how everyone always wanted something from him, and how he was sick and tired of people seeing him only for his money. He wanted to be rid of it all, but he was afraid to start over. I made it easy for him and offered the contract that he was all too happy to sign. I took it all from the drunken fool."

It made a certain kind of sense, but I couldn't understand how it was done. "What makes your contracts so special? I've never heard of someone with the kind of abilities you're talking about." Shouts came from below, and I heard the sound of smashing wood.

"Why don't you find out?" she said softly, her smirk turning into a malevolent grin. She reached into her jacket's inner pocket, extracting a tightly rolled parchment and a quill pen. Yeah, you heard that right. A feather trimmed down to dip into ink and write with. The kind of thing not used in more than a hundred years.

Cissie rolled out the paper on the catwalk, and I could see that it was completely blank. "What would you be willing to sell me, Jack Dahlish? How about that coin around your neck? The thing that started this whole mess for you in the first place. I have a buyer who would part with anything to get his hands on one of the Nine."

She tapped the quill on her chin, as if thinking it over. "In return, I'll give you back your sister and a normal life. You can forget all about the nasty things you've had to deal with over the last decade, and make up for all the times you weren't a good brother. All you have to do is sign, and that life is yours."

She held out the quill, and I looked at it in confusion. Glancing down at the parchment, I saw that it was now covered in letters. A beautiful calligraphy script spelled out the terms of the trade she had just proposed, interspersed with warnings and cautions that all sales are final. Caveat emptor.

"What in the nine hells is that thing?" I asked hoarsely, unable to look away from the parchment. More ringing steps on the steel ladder now, someone moving quickly up to the catwalk.

"Does it matter? I'm offering you the one thing you've been wanting deep in your heart. The thing you dream about and wish for in your quiet moments. Sign the contract, and it *will* happen. You'll go home, and tomorrow or the next day your sister will walk in the door and greet you as if she's only been away on an exciting trip." I could hear grunting, and the slapping sound of a bare fist hitting skin over and over.

I tried to tell myself that she was wrong, that I'd never turn my back on the responsibility I'd accepted as one of the Nine. I tried to tell myself her words were poison, that nothing the woman said could ever be trusted. I tried to tell myself that even if it were possible to bring my sister back to life, I'd be stealing her soul away from whatever restful place it had gone to.

Which is why I was completely shocked to find the quill in my hand. I couldn't even remember reaching out for it, much less taking it. And yet the smooth shaft of it was resting between my fingers, cool to the touch and almost quivering as if it felt excitement at what I was about to do. I watched in horror as I lowered it to the parchment, and it approached the line at the bottom awaiting my signature.

"No!" a rumbling voice cried out. "Jack, don't do it!"

I knew that voice, but the name wouldn't come to me. I was so entranced by the contract in front of me that I couldn't spare the time to figure it out. I shook off the worry, even as a small voice at the back of my brain cried out for me to listen. The quill lowered, until the sharpened tip touched the parchment.

A sharp scream sounded, fading before it was quickly cut off with the sound of something heavy hitting the ground. The catwalk shook, and I heard footsteps running toward me. I dragged my eyes up to look, but Cissie's gaze caught me. Her face was filled with excited anticipation, and there was no worry or concern there at all. I wanted to look away, look beyond her, but I felt myself drawn deeper and deeper into her black eyes.

My hand started to move, slowly scratching along the parchment as I wrote without looking away from the black pools of her eyes. The footsteps behind her got louder, and then a large man loomed up. "Jack, stop!" I couldn't look away to see Nyk's face, but only watch as the triumph filled her eyes.

"Yes!" Cissie screamed. "Now you know why so many people will sign away the things they treasure. The things they value, even if no one else does. And now this belongs to me." Her hand reached eagerly for the silver chain around my neck. I didn't move, except to release the quill to roll on the parchment.

Her fingers touched the delicate silver links, caressing the chain before she wrapped warm fingers under it and began to pull it away from my neck. I lowered my head, helping her goal of removing the coin. Nyk kept saying "no" over and over in absolute horror, and I vaguely wondered why he didn't try to stop her. The coin began to lift, sliding up my chest until it came free of my shirt and was exposed.

Cissie screamed again, this time in pain and anger. Her hand yanked away, releasing the silver chain to fall around my neck once more. I could smell burning flesh, and looked up with a smile to see her fingers still smoking and red. "What is this?" she shrieked at me. "You signed the contract. That coin is mine!"

"Look again," I said calmly, pushing the parchment toward her. Cissie glanced down, examining the signature line and shouted in frustration. Instead of my name, the line was filled with two simple words. *You lose.*

I grabbed the quill from where it still rolled around, holding it tightly in the palm of my hand as I rammed the sharp end up into the soft spot under her jaw. Her mouth was still open with rage spewing out, and I saw the quill enter the bottom of her mouth and slice through her tongue into the soft palette at the top. Frustration turned to pain on her face.

At the same moment, Nyk reached down with a large hand and took hold of her upper arm. He pulled her into the air, turning her with ease to hold her at a level where he could look into her eyes. Her feet were dangling a foot above the catwalk, kicking as she tried to find purchase. I was finally able to look up at my friend, and I saw murder in his eyes.

Nyk took a step, moving closer to the edge of the catwalk. I glanced down, seeing a body in a black suit lying in an expanding pool of blood. I recognized what I could see of the man's face, one of the goons who had been in Billy Wish's office, the man standing by the SUV on that night I thought the Magpie died.

"Don't," I said forcefully. "Don't do it, Nyk. I know you want to, and I really wish I could let you, but it's not the way we need to handle this. That woman is the Magpie, and we need her if we're going to have even a slim hope of making right what's she done through the years." I grabbed the parchment, not surprised to see it was blank once more. Not even a drop of blood marred the smooth white surface. I rolled it up and held it in my hand as I pulled myself up on the railing.

Cissie was still screaming incoherent words, flecks of blood and spittle spraying from her mouth that was held open by the quill. Nyk's hands tightened, the knuckles going white, until I was afraid he would snap her arms with his grip. Finally, he dropped her, and she screamed with rage and pain again as the jarring landing forced her jaw down onto the sharp point of the quill, driving it deeper into her upper palette. Nyk forced her to turn, pulling a pair of plastic wrist cuffs from his back pocket and sliding them over her hands.

Outside, I could hear approaching sirens. I looked over at the bounty hunter, and he shrugged. "When you didn't answer, I called Ollie and told him you were in trouble. Then I burst in and did my best to save you."

"You totally did," I assured him. "I think I was really going to sign that contract before I heard your voice. She promised to give my sister back."

He nodded in sympathy, seeming to hear the tears in the thickness of my voice. "She's in a better place, Jack." Then he pushed the Magpie in front of him and walked away to descend the ladder to the floor below. I wondered how he would get Cissie down with her hands cuffed behind her back, and then snorted a laugh when the big man just flung the woman kicking and screaming over his shoulder before climbing down.

I had a lot of things to think through, especially how close I'd come to giving up the talisman, but I knew I didn't have the time to do it there. Chatterton, the lawyer, was laying on the floor near the wide-open door at the entrance to the warehouse, and I hoped he was just unconscious. The two hooded figures were nowhere to be seen, and I sighed with the knowledge that I'd have to spend time identifying them and tracking them down. The best lead was the last person left below.

Goldblatt was still smoking his cigar, down to a stub now, standing with his hands in his pockets as he watched Nyk descend the ladder. He said a few words to the bounty hunter, too quietly for me to hear, and then turned and sauntered away for a rear exit. He looked up once, raising a hand to tip the brim of his straw hat when our eyes met. I probably should have stopped him, but as the adrenaline left my system, I was feeling too exhausted to even find the energy to speak.

The trap door above me remained closed, and I hoped the big man named Tol was still up there so the cops could round him up. If not, I guessed I could let Nyk handle it for me. If I never saw another black-suited giant in my life, it would be too soon.

By the time I climbed down to the warehouse floor, cops were rushing into the building holding their guns out. I raised my arms at my side to show I was unarmed and had to endure being tossed to the ground and cuffed as more and more of them poured in to secure the building. They left Nyk alone, and I couldn't blame them for that. A couple of uniformed cops took Cissie away from him, though.

Ollie arrived soon after, pointing me out and getting the cuffs removed. "Hell, Jack, you look like shit. More than usual." He was wiping blood from my face, which was still pouring out of the wound on my head.

"She's the one," I said, ignoring his concerns and unable to look away from Cissie. Two paramedics were working to remove the quill from under her chin, but her eyes were locked on mine. I didn't like the gloating I saw in them at that moment. "That's the real Magpie. The woman who killed my sister."

"Holy shit," Ollie breathed, turning to look at her. "And she's still alive? I thought you would have been hell bent for revenge."

"I was," I admitted. "But it wouldn't bring Jen back. I thought her killer was dead ten years ago, and it never really gave me the comfort I'd hoped for. It wouldn't have happened this time, either."

Ollie put a hand on my shoulder and squeezed. "Jack Dahlish, I do believe you're getting a little wiser in your old age." He was grinning at me, and I could hear pride in his voice.

"What's going to happen to her?" I asked, still looking at Cissie. The quill had been removed, and the paramedics were stuffing gauze into her mouth to staunch the bleeding. "She's done all kinds of heinous things, but I don't know how much of it we can prove. Or how much of it we can even reveal outside of the Nox community."

"We'll hold her for forty-eight hours, at least. If nothing else, the detectives are going to want to talk to her about what the hell was going on in here." He glanced over to where Chatterton was laying on a stretcher, bandages being wrapped around his head. The man's eyes were open, but glazed and unfocused. "I guess she has a lawyer present, but I don't know how much good he'll be for at least two or three days. Whatever hit him, it hit hard." We both glanced at Nyk, leaning against the wall with tree trunk arms crossed.

Nyk felt our stares and looked over. He nodded slowly, and I knew he was thinking the same thing I was. Whatever the cops did, we'd have to deal with the Magpie our way in the end. She'd done too much damage to too many lives to let her go free. But we'd reverse as much of it as we could before we took the ultimate step.

Ollie escorted me outside to one of the half dozen ambulances waiting in the street. The night air was alive with flashing red and white lights, and the sound of dozens of police officers setting up yellow tape to block off the crime scene. A female paramedic helped me up into the ambulance, having me lay on the gurney so she could look at the gash in my head. After twenty minutes and a couple of small stitches, I was cleaned up and standing back in the cold night.

Arms encircled my waist, and I looked with surprise to see red hair leaning against my shoulder. "Why do you always get into these situations, Jack? Am I going to have to worry about you every time you're working on a case?"

I wrapped an arm around Karen's shoulders, feeling a satisfied smile creep across my face. "One of the perks of knowing me, I guess."

She turned her luminous green eyes up to my blue ones, and I could see real concern. "As soon as I heard the call on the police scanner, I knew you were involved somehow. Then they called for all these ambulances, and I couldn't help thinking the worst." She closed her eyes, taking a deep breath. "I've never felt so much worry over someone before."

I was opening my mouth to reply when she stretched up to kiss me, our lips meeting. I felt a spark run through my body, and I was reaching to pull her closer when she broke off and hurried back over to the KRSA news van. I was left with conflicting feelings, wondering if I was still misreading things.

Ollie's chuckle from nearby made me whirl to find him leaning against the side of the ambulance. "That woman likes you, Jack. I can't for the life of me figure out why, but she really does." He reached out to slap my arm with the back of his hand, before turning to walk back into the club.

A few minutes later, Nyk came out and motioned with his head for me to follow him. Once we were in his truck, with the engine running so the heaters could warm us, he broke out in a triumphant smile. "We got her," he said.

217

"For now. The cops will question her, but I can't see Cissie giving them anything. Then she'll be out, and I'll be watching my back until we have her again and do what I should have let you do on that catwalk."

"No, Jack. We got her." Nyk looked at me, and then held out his phone. I could see the recording program pulled up, and a short audio file queued up. I was confused, but I reached out to tap the button to play the file. I listened in growing surprise as I heard faint words on the recording.

"Your phone called mine," he explained. "I guess you must have hit the button just before you dropped it. When I answered, I could hear talking but couldn't understand it. I started recording it, and then called Ollie on another phone." He motioned to one laying on the dash, another prepaid cell he must have been keeping stashed in the vehicle. "I edited out all the stuff they couldn't use, and then turned over the bit where she talks about taking Chip's wealth and businesses. They'll be able to follow up on that, and hopefully charge her with theft."

"But he willingly signed the contract."

"So she says, but the poor guy was so drunk he can't even remember any of that night. Diminished capacity, which makes any agreement non-binding. In the human world." He was smiling even wider now. "She might end up in a country club prison, but it'll be a long sentence."

"Huh." I leaned back, enjoying the warmth pouring from the vents. "I guess that's better than nothing. But what are we going to do about the rest of the group in there?"

218

"Another job for another day," the bounty hunter said. "Goldie, who was apparently my employer on this job, assured me the Circle wouldn't be operating in our city for a while. I had to let him leave so he can take leadership and put their operations on hold."

I knew I'd be butting up against this Circle again but had to be thankful for a little breathing room. Knowing the identity of three of the members would give me a good starting point when I did dig into them. It might take a lot of work, but I'd find a way to bring them all down.

Nyk and I sat in his idling truck for over an hour, watching the cops cart away the living and the dead. By midnight, the lights had gone dark and all but two of the police cars had driven away. Those left behind would guard the crime scene until the morning hours, when techs would sweep the exterior for anything that might tie in with what went on inside. Thanks to Ollie, Nyk and I were considered bystanders in the entire thing. Our statements had been taken, and we wouldn't have to worry about answering any more questions.

THEN

I crouched in the brush for hours, watching the police arrive and listening to the officers talking about the strange coincidence of finding a body in the same secluded spot for the second time in a week. When I saw the coroner's van arrive, I decided it was time to get moving before crime scene techs began to comb the area.

Getting through several hundred yards of brushy undergrowth was the easiest part. When I stepped onto a street again, pausing under a streetlight to look down at myself, I found that I was covered in rusty brown splotches of dried blood. A few white bits of bone stood out in the light, and I brushed them off as well as I could. I didn't have another shirt to change into after the coin blew a hole through my other, so I had to find a house with a hose bib in an area that was dark enough for me to crouch and try to wash my shirt and scrub the dried blood from my skin.

Once I felt clean enough, I stumbled through the streets looking for a bus stop. I refused to go toward the one I knew about, not wanting to risk some cop seeing me there and recognizing me from earlier in the week. I was walking with my head down and my backpack held tightly in my hands when a bright light flashed on me for a second. Turning in shock, I saw a police car coasting to the curb.

The door opened, and I saw a middle-aged cop stand and look at me. He shook his head, and then circled around the hood of the car to hold open the passenger door. "Get in, Mr. Dahlish."

I looked at Officer Williams in fear for several seconds before realizing I had no choice. I could take off running, but there was no way I'd escape a man in a car. I didn't even know this area well enough to know where I could run *to*. With my head down, I slid into the car and the door quietly closed.

The officer settled into his own seat, casting a glance in my direction as he put the car in gear and pulled away to drive slowly through the streets. "I had a feeling I might find you around here, once I saw where the body was. I'm guessing that was Billy Wish?"

"Yeah," I said miserably. It was the first time I'd ever seen someone killed, and it had happened only a few feet away from me. The elation that my sister's killer was dead faded quickly as the sick feeling rushed in to take its place. "I didn't do it."

The car was silent for a bit, and then Officer Williams sighed. "No, I didn't expect you had. You don't have the feel of a murderer, Mr. Dahlish."

"Jack. Call me Jack."

"Okay, Jack. Tell me what happened out there. Just between you and me for now."

I debated how much to tell him, and then decided I had to trust him. After all, he could have taken me straight back and turned me over to the detectives who would have been happy to call the case solved and give him a commendation for his quick

221

thinking. I told him everything that had happened since the day my sister's body was found. I even told him about the coin hanging around my neck, and the two birdmen jumping me in the alley.

By the time I was winding down, feeling as if I'd been relieved of a burden I'd not noticed I was carrying, I realized we were driving along the interstate and headed south. I looked out of the window for a while, noting how quiet it looked in the first hour of the new day. "Are you going to take me to the looney bin?"

"No, I don't think I will." Officer Williams sounded as surprised as I did. "I'm not sure why, but for some reason I believe you, Jack. Not one bit of it makes a lick of sense to me, and it sounds like the kind of thing my kids would have dreamed up while playing pretend, but I believe every word of it."

He laughed then, a pleasant rolling sound that made me smile in response. "It sure explains a few reports we saw yesterday about giant hawks flying out of an alley with a spotlight behind them. I can tell you the guys down at the station had a good laugh about that."

The car exited the interstate, onto a feeder road that led towards the downtown district. "Where are we going then?"

"Well, Jack, you mentioned that bartender who helped you out and gave you a place to stay. I thought it might be a good place to take you. After what you just experienced, I guarantee you're going to need a good long sleep. Adrenaline can be a bitch when it finally wears off, like it is right now." I was sure he could see my drooping eyelids, even as I worked to stay alert.

222

It wasn't long before the car stopped at the curb, and I could see a set of stairs down to the Riverwalk a few steps away. He turned to me, holding out his hand. I stared at it for a few seconds, then reached across and met the handshake. "Call me Ollie," he said. "Once you're ready, call me and I'll take you in to make a statement. Not to all of it," he said, raising a hand when he saw I was about to protest. "Just the bits you can tell without being laughed out of the room. Tie this Billy Wish character to your sister's murder, tell them about meeting him in that club and his bodyguards assaulting you in the alley. That will give the detectives a place to start, and they'll question those goons in suits. I'm sure they'll get to the right answer of who killed Billy, even if they don't know the correct reason."

Twenty minutes later, I pushed through the door into Lyon's Den. The bar was crowded with a few dozen other people, drinking alone at the bar or in small groups at the tables set by the opposite wall. Every eye looked up when I entered, a wariness in their expressions that spoke of constant worry that the wrong person would find them. Terrance, sitting at the bar again in his usual spot, was the only one that recognized me. His gaze fell to my chest again, but then rose up to meet my eyes with suspicion. I'd like to say I went over and calmed his worries, but I set a ten-year precedent by ignoring him and looking around for Richard.

The bartender stared at me, a smile blossoming on his lips. He walked over to where I took the stool I'd occupied on my last two visits, the stool that would become like a second home, stopping only long enough to fill a glass with a new

223

microbrewery concoction. As he set it down in front of me, I realized the room was quiet. Everyone was still looking at me.

"What's going on?" I whispered, leaning against the bar.

"Tengu are big blabbermouths," Richard said. "Five minutes after you fought off their attack, the news was spreading through the Nox. You accepted the talisman, Jack, and now they all know you're the newest member of the Nine."

"Oh." I looked around again, taking notice of the expressions that met my gaze. Most were wary, but also respectful. Only a few of the Nox in the room seemed to resent my presence. "I don't even know how I should handle that."

Richard shrugged. "Start a tab and buy a round. That usually works to put people at ease."

"I doubt I have a job after I didn't show up tonight. So it'll be a long time before I could pay a tab." That depressing thought was beginning to settle on me, the prospect of losing another job when I was just starting to get my feet under me again.

"Well, I might have something to help with that." Richard leaned against the bar, pursing his lips for a second. "One of my regulars has been telling me about this series of muggings on the east side of town. Even when a better target is nearby, the muggers always select a Nox. He wants someone to investigate it, but he is justifiably hesitant to take it to the cops. The pay isn't great, but it's about what you were making at your job. If you're interested."

I looked down into my beer, wondering how I could even start to look into something like that. Then I realized I didn't have any better prospects, and I *had* managed to figure out who killed my sister. Maybe I would turn out to be a good investigator. Maybe I could earn the responsibility that came with the coin hanging around my neck. I grunted and nodded.

"Next round is on Dahlish," Richard called out, winking at me as he stepped away to begin filling orders.

NOW

A week after the events in the warehouse, I was sitting in my office reading another of the many reference books I'd been poring through. The information seemed to confirm that I had come across a previously unknown Relic, imbued with a fragment of energy left over from when the god Sancus was at the height of his power. The Romans worshiped him as the god of trust, honesty, and oaths. They signed contracts in his name, trusting that the god would hold both parties compliant to the agreements.

Whatever it was, the parchment was safely locked away in my very secure storage closet. The building could crumble around me, and that steel-lined closet would survive with everything inside intact. It was where I kept anything I felt was too dangerous to be out in the world.

My butt was starting to hurt from sitting in the thinly padded seat of my client chair, and I shut the lid on my laptop to look toward my supremely comfortable swivel chair. Penny was sitting there, drawing with crayons on a large pad that lay on my desk. Every now and then, she would push the chair around in a circle, giggling with joy as she did it.

Anna had dropped the girl off a few hours earlier, asking me to watch her for a while. Penny's father, Michael, had finally gotten his deal approved with the state's attorney. In exchange for testifying against the owner of the garage he'd worked at, the man who had coerced him into participating in a string of bank robberies with other employees, Michael was granted a reduced sentence and being released with time served.

I looked at my watch and realized he must be leaving the courthouse soon. Anna had spent two years convinced the father of her child, a man she loved, would never come back to them. I could only imagine the joy she was feeling. Emilio, Michael's brother, had to be feeling that same joy. He'd devoted the last few years of his life to keeping Anna and Penny safe and provided for.

"Hey, munchkin. Want to walk down to the river and see if we can find some ducks?"

"Ducks!" Penny cried, dropping the crayon on her quickly forgotten drawing and bouncing out of the chair. I had to almost wrestle with her to get us both into coats, and then was dragged down the hallway to the elevators. The whole way to the River- walk, Penny talked about how much she wanted to pet a duck and take it home with her. I could only laugh, reveling in her simple joy and passion in the moment.

I hope you've enjoyed this second book in the Dahlish series. Jack will return soon in Dark Deception, where he learns that it's harder to tell the difference between friends and enemies than he always thought.

Read on for a short story that takes place soon after Jack first put the coin around his neck. He is still trying to get used to the strange life he's found himself in when a new friend calls him for help.

Strange Encounters

I pushed a curved chip into my mouth, crunching down on it as I stared through the windshield of my car at the motel across the street. A car would occasionally pass by on the street, but at two in the morning the traffic was very light. My gaze was locked on the door to room 17, where I'd seen my target enter half an hour earlier.

A yawn snuck up on me, and I raised a hand to cover my mouth. This was my third long night in a row at my "day" job, while also running down leads on Nox jobs when I should have been getting more sleep. I couldn't complain too much, though, since a friend had called in favors to get me the job working for a private investigation firm in town.

In the days after I watched my sister's killer die, it had been almost impossible for me to return to my old job working a complaints line for a national retailer. With the Relic that now hung around my neck, I felt a calling to do something more. To really help the Nox of San Antonio, I needed a P.I. license. To get one of those I needed experience in the field. Six months experience, to be exact. I was in the middle of my second.

The door of the room I was watching opened a crack. I hastily put the can of chips down on the passenger seat, and then grabbed the camera with the telephoto lens. Company equipment, so I had to be extra careful with it to make sure I didn't break anything.

I managed to get half a dozen good shots of a middle-aged man as he left the room with his arm around a woman who was far too young for him. I highly doubted she was much over eighteen, if she were at all. That wasn't what I was on his trail for, though. His soon-to-be-ex-wife just needed proof of his infidelity to ensure she got custody of their young children.

The man got into a fairly new sports car, revving the engine as he pulled out of the motel lot. I could only shake my head in disgust at the meaningless display. His prostitute turned to walk the other direction, returning to her corner to wait for the next john to pull up. One of the things I'd learned during this stake-out was that her pimp booked a couple of rooms at the motel every night, so his girls had a relatively safe place to take their customers. It had the side benefit of limiting the time they were away from their nearby posts.

I scrolled through the pictures on the camera's small digital screen, smiling at the one where the man had one arm around the prostitute's shoulder while his other was reaching up to feel a breast. Coupled with a shot of the pair entering the room half an hour earlier, it was all the proof our client would need. I flipped open my phone, pressing the button I had programmed to dial my boss. It went straight to voicemail, which wasn't unusual so late at night. "Raleigh, I've got the photos for the Tucker case. I'll upload them to the server as soon as I get home. Call me tomorrow if I'm needed for anything."

230

Ten minutes later, I stumbled through the door of my crappy one-bedroom apartment. The complex was in a shady part of town, but it was a vast improvement from the shelters I'd had to sleep in for several weeks as I struggled to get back on my feet.

My laptop was on the kitchen counter, already displaying a logon screen. It was another piece of company equipment issued to me when I'd been hired, with an admonition to take care of it. It took me several minutes to plug in the camera, download the pictures, then upload the best ones into the company website where my boss could access them later that morning.

With the work done, I shut the laptop lid and peeled off my clothes as I walked into the bedroom. I had an old mattress laying on the floor, and I plopped down onto it with a sigh of contentment. Less than a minute later, I was snoring.

* * * * *

The ringing of my phone woke me several hours later. I blinked my eyes as I patted around the floor beside my mattress. When I finally remembered that I'd left the phone on the counter beside the laptop and camera, I groaned and rolled to stand up. Before I reached the kitchen, the ringing stopped.

A voice mail indicator was on the small display, so I flipped open the phone and pressed the key to check it. It was short, just a few words asking me to call back when I had a chance. The thought of returning to my mattress flitted across my mind, but I owed him too much to not call back right away.

"Hey, Ollie," I said, once he'd picked up the call after a single ring.

"Good morning, Jack. Did I wake you?"

"Yeah, but it's okay. What's going on?"

Ollie hesitated before plunging onward with his request. "Can you come meet me at a scene? I'm getting a strange feeling about this one, and I want you to look at it."

I checked the clock on the stove, mourning the hours of sleep I had looked forward to. "Sure. What's the address?"

It took twenty minutes to get across town to the address Ollie provided. Traffic was getting heavier as I drove, and I stopped for a very large coffee at a gas station. Much cheaper than a fancy coffee shop, and it woke me up just as much.

As I pulled to the curb behind a patrol car, Ollie hurried over to greet me. I guess the rusty old Saturn I'd barely been able to afford when I started the private investigation job stood out in that neighborhood. "Jack, thanks for coming." He shook my hand, his grip strong and confident. "I hope I'm not bothering you for no reason. I just saw something here that made me remember our conversation. You know, the one that night after the pond."

He was referring to the night that Billy Wish died, the man who'd killed my sister. Ollie had found me wandering the neighborhood afterward, and on the drive downtown I spilled out the story of the supernatural Nox that I'd just learned existed earlier in the day when I was attacked by a couple of bird-like tengu. For some reason, he'd believed me.

"What happened?"

He motioned for me to follow as he started walking towards a knot of men and women ahead. "Several calls came in around four this morning from people reporting the sound of gunshots. Anywhere from six to twenty, according to witnesses."

We ducked under the yellow crime scene tape that was blocking the concrete walkway that led to a modest two-story home. Aside from the lack of decorations, it was the sort of home most families would be happy to live in. The uniformed officer guarding the door gave me a nasty look, but she didn't say anything as Ollie ushered me into the house.

The first body was in the hallway. He looked to be a teenager on the cusp of adulthood, shot twice in the back as he tried to run away. That wasn't what had drawn Ollie's attention, however. He knelt next to the body, lifting the sheet that had been placed over the kid's legs.

I retched when I saw the ragged tears in the flesh before he dropped the sheet quickly. "Something ate him?"

"Started to," Ollie said with a nod. "The other bodies look the same." He turned to look at a stairway, with a hall that continued past it to another room where I could see the flash of cameras documenting the scene. "Best as we can tell, these kids were cooking meth in this house. Someone surprised them this morning, killed all four, and took their stash."

He ushered me out of the house before someone spotted us and raised hell. In the front yard, I sucked in clean air as I tried to get the image of the bite marks out of my head. Aside from watching my sister's killer die, this was the first time I'd been in the presence of death. I didn't like it.

"The detectives think it was a rival group," Ollie said quietly, standing close to me. He rubbed a finger over his mustache as he talked, a gesture that was common when he was thinking deeply about something.

"Jesus," I said in shock, patting my stomach in an attempt to banish the queasiness. "This is awful, but why do you think there's something supernatural here?"

"They're saying dogs attacked the bodies, but I don't buy it, Jack. Predatory animals have narrow jaws, but those bite marks came from something wider. Like a human mouth." He grimaced, checking to be sure no one might have overheard. "Isn't there some way you can check if it might have been one of those noxious or whatever you called them?"

"Nox," I said absently, reaching up to touch the coin through my shirt. Richard had told me the talisman granted its wearer the ability to detect the presence of Filii Nox, but so far I'd been unable to figure out how that worked. I owed it to Ollie to try, though.

I closed my eyes, trying to focus on the coin. These days, I barely even felt it against my skin unless I was thinking about it. The coin was so light that it would have been more of a burden to wear a feather. My fingers circled the edge of it, as I tried to force it to work for me. Commands soon turned to pleading.

When I felt the first traces of nausea, I thought it was nothing more than a return of what I'd felt when I saw the blood and exposed flesh on the body. I groaned, opening my eyes as I prepared to tell Ollie that I couldn't help.

I paused, my mouth hanging open as I looked around the yard we were standing in. A sickly green fog had crept in while my eyes were closed, and a gust of wind blew the smell of really bad body odor my way. "Someone needs to hit the showers," I said as I raised a hand to pinch my nose.

Ollie gave me a strange look. "What are you talking about, Jack?"

"You don't smell that? And what's up with this fog? Strange color."

He put a hand on my shoulder, bending forward to look at me with concern. "There's no fog, Jack. Cloudless day," he said, looking up at the slowly brightening morning sky.

A sky I could see perfectly when I followed the direction of his gaze. "Huh," I said, looking around at the green fog again. It disappeared *into* the house. I took a few steps back toward the door, where the officer on guard raised her hand to stop me from entering again. There was no need, since I could see the fog thickly circling the body inside before it split to go up the stairs and into the room at the back of the house.

"You really don't see it?" I asked when I rejoined Ollie. "And you don't smell that god-awful stench?"

"No," he said, shaking his head. "Look, I know Raleigh has you working pretty hard. I shouldn't have called you in just because an old man got a weird feeling in his gut." Ollie had been the one to get me the job with the small agency, vouching for me even though we'd known each other only a few days at that point.

"Wait," I said, reaching up to rub the back of my neck. "I'm really seeing green fog, Ollie. I think… maybe this is how the coin works? Richard said it would reveal 'traces' of the Nox, so maybe that's what I'm seeing."

The nausea was growing stronger with each passing minute. I thought it might have been the horrible stench that grew stronger when I walked into the fog. It had grown to the point that I couldn't take it any longer, and I squeezed my eyes closed as I begged my body not to vomit. In an instant, the nausea faded away.

When I opened my eyes again, the green fog had disappeared. The air was fresh in my nostrils, and I sucked it in greedily. I was feeling very confused, but more certain than ever that I'd just detected a Nox presence somehow. Not that it told me anything.

Ollie didn't look as convinced when I explained. "I know my eyes start to see some strange things when I'm overly tired."

"No, it was definitely there. The fog or whatever went into the house, around the body, and toward the other areas where I'm betting people were killed. The smell was attached to it, somehow."

"Like perfume?" Ollie asked with a snort. "They left their essence behind for you to track?"

"Yes! Just like that," I said happily. Essence, I liked that word.

"Hmm," Ollie rubbed his mustache again, the bristly black hairs scraping over his finger. "If that's what it was, then this isn't a human killer, is it?"

"Well, not entirely human," I said cautiously. "I can't see just one person killing four guys, even if they were just teenagers."

"True. One of them seemed to be going for a gun that was inside a drawer in the bedroom. He was only steps away when he was dragged down by whatever took a bite out of him." Ollie shook his head sadly.

"Maybe I can follow the trail," I said musingly, stroking the coin as I tried to bring that essence back into focus. I was holding my breath as I strained in an attempt to force it to come back. After a minute I had to finally gasp in a breath. "Or not. I can't get it to come back."

"You're trying too hard," Ollie said with a chuckle. "Your face turned a bright red, Jack. Reminded me of my kids when they were little and would hold their breath trying to make me buy them candy."

I glared at him but couldn't resist a laugh of my own at the image. I took a deep breath, then released it slowly as I closed my eyes and concentrated on the coin again.

"That's it," Ollie said soothingly. "Breathe in. And out. Don't make it happen, let it come on its own.

"Breathe in.

"Breathe out."

His voice was almost hypnotic, and I let myself fall into the gentle rhythm of the deep breaths. When the nausea came roaring back, I couldn't help but feel a tiny amount of triumph.

My eyes opened on the green fog, which looked to be thinner than it had been several minutes earlier. I followed it from the doorway of the house, along the concrete path, to the sidewalk. It turned there, heading northeast.

"This way," I said to Ollie, as he followed closely behind me. We started walking, making it to the end of the block. I paused there, straining to find the essence trail. "It disappears here," I said. "The green essence dies off a few feet into the road."

Ollie was examining the sidewalk and road. "Maybe they got into a vehicle?"

"No, I don't think so. The trail doesn't just cut off, it gets ragged and torn. Like it faded away really quickly beyond the sidewalk."

"As if the traffic blew it away," Ollie murmured. That made sense when I considered it. Even though I couldn't see the green fog without the assistance of the coin, perhaps the human world still had an effect on it.

To be sure, I crossed the street to look for the trail again. I thought I saw small patches of it, but it was hard to be sure. My nose was still full of the body odor stench, and I couldn't tell if that were just memory or something fresh invading my senses.

"At least we know a Nox was involved," I said when I rejoined Ollie.

"I suppose." He didn't sound reassured. I couldn't blame him, since we knew little more than we had before I somehow detected the Nox essence. Less, really, since there were now even more questions to answer. "I'd better get back to the crime scene. I'll let you know what the detectives find, Jack. Thanks for coming out."

"Any time, Ollie. You know that." We shook hands again, and he strolled toward the taped-off house with his head down while I walked back to my car. The door squealed as I opened it to slide behind the wheel.

*   *   *   *   *

I might not have been able to track the supernatural creature that had been at the crime scene, but I felt sure I had enough information to at least narrow down what it was. I'd spent a lot of time in the library in the weeks after I came into possession of the coin, so I knew which sections to visit to learn about the myths and legends that often contained quite a bit of truth about the Nox species they related to.

The only thing I couldn't find was anything relating to the green fog or horrible smell. In the days when the old stories were passed down through tales around the hearth, the Nox hadn't hidden their true appearance from the world. They had been viewed with respect, in most cases, even if it was tinged with fear or revulsion. The people who had worn one of the nine coins that existed in the world had not put their own experiences down. At least, nowhere that I'd been able to find.

By the end of my research, I had few ideas of what kind of creature might have been present at the crime scene. It was something that ate flesh, but it wasn't uncontrollably ravenous in the way a zombie would be. Not that I'd know where to start to look for any of the possibilities. I was still new to the supernatural world.

In fact, there was only one place I knew of in San Antonio that I could be guaranteed to find Nox. After I left the library, I parked in a lot a few blocks from the Riverwalk. The late summer crowds were heavy, but I was content to move at the slow pace they set.

It was not even eleven in the morning when I pulled open the door for Lyon's Den, but I knew I'd find the owner and bartender at his post. Richard Lyon never left the establishment, as far as I could tell, and he only retreated into his attached apartment to sleep during the few hours the bar was closed.

"Jack," he said in greeting, as I dropped down onto the stool I'd unconsciously claimed as my own. It was on the short end of the L-shaped bar, near the wall where I could watch everyone else in the establishment on busy nights. There was only the two of us at the moment.

Richard grabbed a glass from a stack behind the bar and stuck it under a tap to fill it with a local beer. He got a couple of kegs each week from a different microbrewery, a rotating selection that I'd come to anticipate.

"What's on your mind, Jack?" he asked as he slid the beer across to me. I told him about my experience at the crime scene that morning, the essence trail I'd seen and smelled. Richard pursed his lips. "That could be how the coin works."

"You're not sure? You told me it could help me detect Nox through their disguises."

"I'm just working from the information I've picked up from others who have worn the coins through the years," he said with a shrug. "I've never experienced it myself."

I took a sip of the beer, tasting blackberries under the hops. "Did they talk about feeling nauseous, too? The entire time I could see the fog, I felt like I was about to vomit."

Richard shook his head. "You have to understand, Jack, it's not something the Nine really talk about outside of themselves. People who have Relics are naturally secretive."

Relics were objects imbued with the Chaos energy that had formed the universe and created the first gods who later produced the Filii Nox. The coin I wore around my neck, and the other eight just like it, were powerful Relics.

"Are you sure the last guy didn't leave behind a journal or something, to tell his successor how to use this thing?"

Albert Placencia, the man who had worn the coin before it came to me, was killed five years earlier while trying to clean out a nest of rabid vampires. It had taken a year for other members of the Nine to finish the job and recover his body, and by then the coin had disappeared. When it turned up years later, it was in a package sent to me by my sister to keep it out of the hands of those who would keep it hidden away.

241

"If he did, I wouldn't know where to look for it. Sorry, Jack."

"Not your fault," I muttered. "I just wish there were some way to contact one of the other people who have a coin. There has to be a better way to learn than trial and error."

Richard made a sympathetic sound. He'd met others who carried the coins before, but that had been rare occasions as they passed through town. Every sizable city had at least one place like the Den, where the Nox were welcomed and even allowed to shed their human disguises from time to time.

"You said the place was a meth lab?"

"That's what Ollie told me. I didn't get to see much more than the entryway."

"I know someone who might have an idea of what you're up against. Come back around six tonight?" Richard was a human like me, but the Nox had come to accept and trust him. As a bartender, he heard a lot of the stories told over drinks.

"That'll work," I said, taking a deep drink of the beer before standing up. "Put it on my tab."

*　*　*　*　*

After a quick lunch, I spent the afternoon at the agency I was working for. I had to type up a report on my stake-out of the previous evening so it could be sent to our client along with the best photos. There was still some paperwork to be done to finish off a couple of other cases I'd been part of, as well. Even better, my latest weekly paycheck was waiting for me at the reception desk.

I stopped by the bank to deposit it on the way downtown. With a small sheet of paper showing my new bank balance, I had to sit in the car for a few minutes until the smile finally faded from my lips. I'd just gone over three figures for the first time in over four months. There was still a ton of hospital debt to be paid off, but I was in better shape than ever.

When I reflected that I was in such good shape because I had only myself to pay for, sadness crept over me. I would have given anything to have my sister back, even if it meant struggling to stretch a paycheck to cover the bills for two people.

Most of that melancholy was gone by the time I'd parked and walked along the Riverwalk again to enter Lyon's Den. The bar was packed with a dinner crowd, and I was faintly surprised to find my normal stool unoccupied even though there were several people standing against the wall because they didn't have anywhere to sit.

Richard spotted me immediately, waving for me to sit before he turned and walked to the opposite end of the bar. He bent to talk to someone there, a small figure that I couldn't make out in the dim lighting. After a few minutes, that person gave a somewhat grudging nod.

When she stood up from her stool, I got my first look at the young woman Richard had been speaking with. She seemed to be around my age of twenty-four, maybe a few years younger. A foot shy of my six-foot height, with long dark blonde hair and eyes that glowed with a faint reddish tinge. She walked around the bar, coming to a stop several feet away from me. The look on her face said she was trying to decide whether to keep going forward, or to push through the door at her back to escape into the early evening crowds.

She took a few steps forward. "You're the one called Dahlish? The guy who wears the coin?"

"That's me. You want a drink?" I slid off the stool, waving for her to take it.

She shook her head to both offers. "What do you want to know?"

I looked at the man who was sitting on the stool next to mine, and then jerked my head toward the corner of the room. The woman was hesitant, but she followed. We'd have a modicum of privacy there. "Did Richard tell you what I'm looking for?"

"No, he just said I could help myself by helping you."

I told her about the people killed at the house that had been a meth lab. Her eyes hardened as I spoke, and I knew instantly that she had information that was connected in some way. It was an instinct I'd started to develop in my work as a private investigator, one that would come in very handy in the years to come.

"Something about this attack is familiar to you, isn't it?"

The young woman glanced away, and I look in the direction of her gaze to see Richard nod his head slowly. She sighed as she turned back to me. "If I tell you this, you're not going to use it against me, right?"

I tried to smile reassuringly. "I promise, it'll stay between us. I don't even know your name."

She bit her lip for a few moments, then seemed to come to a decision. Her face flickered for a moment, and bristly fur appeared around a black button nose and eyes that were an even brighter shade of red. Just as quickly, her human features returned.

"I work as a runner for a group of marijuana growers. We operate out of a house south of downtown, where a lot of our product funnels through from the farms to the dealers." She darted her eyes around to make sure no one was paying too close attention. "A week ago, this crew hit our house. Three of them, carrying Glocks or whatever. They shot everyone in the house, even this nice old lady who would pick up a small bag of pot every week for her arthritis.

"We had them on our cameras, though. Getting hit was something we were prepared for, so we ponied up for a great surveillance system. Not like we could go to the cops, but we could handle the thieves ourselves." She snorted a contemptuous laugh. "That was the plan, anyway.

"These guys were human, but they had one of us with them. On a chain, man." She shook her head in disgust. "After everyone was dead, they let this one loose. He *ate* chunks out of my friends. Just ripped into them and chewed flesh and muscle like it was nothing." Her eyes took on a distant look, her lips pulling back in revulsion.

"You said he was one of 'us'. Does that mean he was a Nox?"

She nodded.

"Do you know what kind he was?"

"No doubt about it. I've seen them before, years ago when I was a kid."

"What was he?"

She crinkled her nose in disgust. "A ghoul."

* * * * *

After I got home, I did a quick internet search on the mythology around ghouls. They were described as eaters of the dead, subsisting entirely on human flesh. Often found in cemeteries, according to the myths, which would have been like a buffet for them in the days before we stuffed our recently deceased full of chemicals.

When I called Ollie, he was leaving work. I heard the dinging from his car before he closed the door. "A what? Are you messing with me, Jack?"

"A ghoul. I have a witness from a previous attack. Well, their cameras witnessed it and she saw it after the fact."

"This witness was one of your supernatural creatures?"

"A Nox, yeah. Part of a group that has been growing pot and selling it out of a house on the south side." I told him the story I'd gotten from the woman.

"I remember hearing about that. It was ruled to be an attack from rival dealers."

"Has a determination been made on today's murders?"

I could hear Ollie wince through the phone. "Yeah, an attack from rival dealers."

"Sounds like a convenient catch-all solution," I said wryly. "What do they say about the chunks ripped out of each victim?"

"Pit bull," Ollie said with a bemused chuckle.

"I guess I can't complain too much. I'd much rather the cops get lazy than keep digging and find a Nox at the bottom of the pile."

"They're not lazy," Ollie growled. I knew his anger wasn't directed at me, though. "They're working within the system in place. The brass push for closure, and some drug dealers killed in a meth lab aren't worth the resources a good investigation would need."

"Okay, I'm not going to debate policy and budgets with you." I was smiling as I said it, knowing how passionate Ollie could be about the perceived problems with the department that he loved. "I was calling because my source also gave me a location where she thinks this group is holed up."

"Why didn't you lead with that?" Ollie's engine started, and I heard him pull the seat belt across his body before it clicked in. "I'll be at your place in ten."

It only took him eight minutes to get to my apartment. Years of knocking on doors and taking witness statements put him in the habit of banging on a door quite loudly. It shook the walls of my cheap apartment. I walked out, locking the door behind me.

"We'll take my car," I said. "It'll blend in better." Ollie started to protest, but a raised eyebrow put an end to it. He drove an old Crown Victoria that had been a police unit for several years before it was replaced. Even though it was a personal car now, it still looked enough like a cop car to spook criminals who would be looking out for any sign of the police. My old Saturn wouldn't be noticed unless we were driving through nicer parts of town than we were headed for.

The young woman at the Den hadn't given me an address, but more of a location to look in. A neighborhood that encompassed several blocks of houses that were fifty or more years old and looked like they hadn't been properly cared for through the last half of that. Broken down vehicles were parked in yards which were choked with weeds.

Amazingly, though, it was one of the few areas of San Antonio that was known to be off limits for dealers of the various illicit substances. The woman said it was because the group I was after had scared everyone away from their hideout, to make sure the police didn't have a reason to come through this part of town.

Ollie eyed the houses with a sadness I hadn't expected. "These people deserve better, Jack. They work just as hard as you and me, but it's almost impossible for them to break out of this level of poverty."

The sun was low on the horizon when I pulled to the curb. I'd done a full circuit of the streets, finding nothing that was an obvious sign of killers living in a specific house. There was one thing left to try, and I put my fingers on the coin as I closed my eyes and started taking steady breaths.

When I felt the nausea set in, I knew I was now able to see the supernatural world. I opened my eyes to look for any trace of the green fog I'd seen at the crime scene. The street was clear, with nothing out of the norm.

I put the car in gear and pulled away from the curb to drive slowly as I fought the urge to vomit. I turned at the next inter-section, then again to drive in an S shape through the neighbor-hood. Ollie glanced at me a couple of times, but he was pre-ceptive enough not to ask questions.

The nausea was growing harder to control, and I was about to pull myself out of the strange state that let me see Nox es-sences. Just before I did, we turned onto the last street. The green fog filled a yard halfway down the block, growing thicker around the door of the house. Tendrils of it were escaping through cracks in windows, as well.

"That's the place," I said through gritted teeth as we rolled past.

"You're sure?" Ollie asked, doubt in his tone.

"Positive. If you could see it the way I can, you would be, too."

We were silent as I turned at the next corner and parked out of sight from anyone inside the house. I dropped my supernat-ural sight, taking deep breaths as my stomach started to calm down. Once I felt that the slightest movement wouldn't send me retching beside the street, I pushed open my door.

Ollie followed, and we stood together on the sidewalk in the warmth of a late summer Texas evening. The sky was streaked with orange and red, but it would take a few hours for the sun's heat to dissipate. "How do you walk around in that?" I asked, eying the windbreaker he was wearing over a light bulletproof vest.

"I'd rather sweat and live than be cool and die," Ollie said with a glint in his eye. "I offered you my spare."

He had, and I'd turned it down immediately. If guns came out, I planned to get far away as quickly as possible. Call me a coward, but I had a healthy appreciation for breathing and knew my limits. The only weapon I carried was a small pocketknife. The heavy flashlight I pulled from the trunk of my car was probably more deadly, a solid foot of black metal encasing the large D batteries that powered it.

Ollie, on the other hand, was carrying his off-duty weapon. The .45 caliber pistol was holstered in the small of his back, covered by the light windbreaker. I'd seen him draw it from that position before, and it would take only a few seconds for him to have it out and pointed at a threat.

"Let's go," he said, nodding for me to lead the way.

We walked along the sidewalk with measured steps, looking like nothing more than random people out for a bit of exercise if anyone happened to notice us. As we walked past the house, I grunted and tilted my head, so Ollie knew which one had drawn my attention.

The windows were dark, but there was a flicker of light coming from the backyard. It could have been someone watching TV in a back room. We continued past the house, looping around the block.

"No car in the drive," Ollie muttered once we were off that street and looping around the block.

"I saw a shed in the back that looks big enough for a car. Do we have any idea what they drove when they attacked the meth house?"

"Witnesses disagree on the details. Could be a dark truck or an SUV. Either would be a tight fit for that small shed."

As we turned onto the street for a second pass of the house, the bright lights of a vehicle flashed across our faces as it turned onto the street at the far end. I raised an arm to shield my eyes as Ollie ducked his head. The lights finally dimmed, and when my dazzled vision cleared, I saw a black SUV parked in the short driveway beside the house I knew the ghoul inhabited.

"Keep walking," Ollie muttered, his lips barely moving. I felt his hand on my arm, urging me to move faster. After we turned off the street again, he pulled me over to a fence that would block us from view.

"That must be them," I said, trying to edge forward and look at the SUV.

Ollie pulled me back. "It was. Two men exited the vehicle and approached the house. A woman opened the door to let them inside."

I looked at him in amazement. "You caught all of that? You weren't even looking at them."

"You learn to use your peripheral vision in my job," he said with a quick smile. "Shifty subjects always do incriminating things when they think you aren't looking."

251

"What do we do now?" I asked. "We know this is them. Should we call the detective in charge of the case."

"*You* know it's them," Ollie said with a cautious tone. "How could you prove it to anyone else?"

I opened my mouth but couldn't find anything to say. He had an excellent point. If I started talking about green fog leading me to the murderers, I'd get laughed out of the room. I could share what the woman at the Den had told me, but I doubted she was going to come forward to share her group's video feeds showing the people who had hit their illegal stash house.

"We can't just sit on them and wait for them to attack someone else."

"Won't have to," Ollie said quietly, waving me forward to peer around the edge of the fence.

The door of the house was open, and two men were walking back to the SUV. A moment later, a squat woman appeared in the doorway. She was holding a thick chain, pulling hard on it. The creature at the end resembled a man, but one who had been beaten hard with the ugly stick. The end of his nose had been chopped off at some point, and his lips were pulled up from scars that crossed his face. Stringy black hair fell over his eyes, only falling back when he raised his face to sniff the air.

"What the hell is that thing?" Ollie asked in disgust.

"Ghoul," I said, feeling the same revulsion at the sight of it. Even from half a block, we could pick up on the waves of utter wrongness that seemed to pour off the creature.

"They're leaving," Ollie said. "Come on, we need to get back to your car before we lose them." He took off at a brisk jog, and I rushed to keep up with him. We ran down the next street over, reaching the far side just as the SUV drove past. Ollie put on more speed, and I gasped to keep up.

We piled into my car, and I jammed the key into the ignition. The tires squealed as I pulled a quick U-turn, and I pressed the pedal to the floor in an attempt to catch up.

"Turn!" Ollie shouted, pointing left. I barely made the corner, two wheels going up on the curb and then dropping back to the street again a moment later. Red taillights were in sight for only a second before they turned a couple of blocks ahead. I followed, breathing a sigh of relief as the SUV passed under a streetlight and I got reassurance that we were following the correct vehicle.

Ollie was tense beside me, one hand out to grip the dash as he frowned at the SUV that I kept at least five car lengths in front of us. "I don't like this, Jack. Where are they going?"

"Maybe hitting another stash house?"

He shook his head. I could tell there was an internal debate raging on whether he should call it in, but he was hampered by the same issues that would have presented if I'd tried to report these people to the cops. "If I see so much as a crowbar in one of their hands, I'm calling for backup."

"Backup would be nice," I said. I'd been thinking for the last several weeks that I needed to make more friends who would be willing to back me up when dangerous situations came up. Like the one I was currently in. Finding people who were accustomed to this kind of situation wasn't exactly simple, though.

When the SUV finally turned off the street, they pulled through a gate in a metal fence, into a row of small warehouses. Solid brick walls faced the street, but roll-up metal doors would be on the other side of the buildings. I drove past the warehouses, pulling into a run-down strip mall parking lot next door. A small Mexican café was open, with half a dozen cars parked nearby.

Ollie and I climbed out of the car again, looking warily toward the high fence that surrounded the warehouse complex. "No way we're getting over that," I said.

"We won't have to," Ollie said, pointing to where another vehicle was pulling up to the gate. He walked quickly in that direction, and I was only a few steps behind. We were halfway to the gate when it rolled open and the car pulled through. I could hear the rattle of the machinery as it started to close behind them.

I made it through the fence only a second before it closed, hurrying to stand beside Ollie against the side of the nearest building. "We're too exposed here," he whispered, leading me toward the narrow path between two of the warehouses.

The shadows there were deep enough to keep us hidden from casual observers. It also turned out to be the perfect place to observe our quarry from. The SUV was parked in front of a warehouse facing us, at the rear of the complex. The wide metal door was rolled up, exposing a large space filled with storage racks that contained bundles wrapped in plastic. As we

254

watched, the car we'd followed into the facility pulled up beside the SUV.

I was amazed to see a pair of men exit the car, prototypical gangbangers down to the facial tattoos and pistols shoved into the front of their baggy jeans. "This can't be where they're storing the stolen drugs. Right?"

"Why not?" Ollie whispered with a chuckle. "I bet the records for that unit would be in some false name that we could never trace back to these guys. No security cameras on the gate, and I don't see any at the corners of the buildings. An area with regular traffic where someone pulling in late at night or early in the morning wouldn't stand out. Perfect place to hide them."

One of the two men we'd seen at the house approached the newcomers, wearing tight blue jeans with a dark polo shirt tucked in. He was clean cut, the kind of man you could see on every street in the world and never pay them much notice. It was a stark contrast to the gang members he faced. I craned my head, but I didn't see the other man or the woman with the ghoul on a chain leash.

"Yo, man, we gonna do this?" one of the gangbangers said, throwing his hands up wildly as he spoke. "Show us the goods, and we show you the cash."

"My associate is retrieving the packages you are interested in now. We will need to see the cash first, gentlemen, to verify that you are able to afford what we are offering." I raised my eyebrows on hearing his voice, smooth tones that indicated an education. Not the thuggish tones I'd expected.

"This better be good stuff," the spokesman for the gang-bangers said, waving for his companion to retrieve a large duffel bag from the trunk of their car. The bag was tossed down in front of the spokesman, and he knelt to pull back the zipper. Bundles of currency almost spilled out.

"Very good. I believe we can continue." The man in the polo shirt turned his head, issuing a sharp whistle. Several moments later, the woman appeared in a forklift to drop a pallet with a hundred or so tightly wrapped bundles near the warehouse door. "One hundred kilos of marijuana, as requested."

The gangbangers shared a stunned look, and the spokesman stepped forward to lift one of the bundles. He produced a knife from his pocket, slitting open the package to hold it up to his nose as he breathed in the scent. "That's good shit, yo!"

"The product comes from a variety of suppliers, but I assure you it is all top quality."

"Better be," the gangbanger said, a challenge in his tone that was ignored.

I heard the crunch of footsteps on loose gravel behind us, and Ollie reached out to push me down. "Look what we have here," a voice said from behind him. "Peeping Tom found a bit more than he expected?"

Ollie nudged me with his foot, and I realized he was telling me to move behind a crate that lay against the wall. I was in deeper shadows there, and whoever had snuck up on us must not have seen me. "You don't want to do this," he said in his deep voice, his tone calm and even.

"All I'm doing is confronting a trespasser. Move."

Ollie walked past me with his hands held out at his sides. The second man from the SUV was behind him, a small gun pressed against his back. As soon as they passed, I quickly moved forward to watch them cross the open space between the rows of warehouses.

The gangbangers looked up, and their hands immediately went to the guns in their waistbands. "Trevor, look what I found," the man behind Ollie called.

The one called Trevor didn't appear concerned at the development. He only smiled, waving for his partner to lead Ollie into the warehouse. "Darla's pet was starting to get hungry. Nice of this gentleman to volunteer to feed it." They shared a nasty laugh, while the gangbangers shot each other an uncomfortable glance.

Trevor noticed, turning his attention back to them. "Perhaps you'd like to stay and watch? A demonstration of what will happen should you ever fail to pay."

"Naw, man. We good." The gangbanger spokesman jerked his head and the two of them made quick work of loading the packages into the trunk of their car. In the couple of minutes that it took them to complete the process, I ran in a crouch across the open pavement, darting behind anything that would provide cover.

By the time they were backing their car away from the open warehouse door, I was only a dozen feet away. I couldn't see much of the warehouse space, and I wasn't able to see where Ollie was. I could hear a grumbling, growling sound on the other side of the wall, though, and I knew the ghoul was close to me.

Trevor waited until the car was out of sight, then turned to the warehouse with an anticipatory grin. He pressed a button on the wall as he passed, and the metal door started to lower slowly, clanking loudly as it rattled in the slots.

I used that noise to cover my own quick steps as I crossed to lean against the wall just beside the shrinking opening. I poked my head inside, catching a glimpse of a walled space on the other side of the bricks from where I'd been crouching. Trevor was disappearing through a door there.

With none of the others in sight, I ducked into the warehouse before the door was too low. Under the noise of the final rattles as it hit the ground, I approached the door into the closed-off space.

"Who are you?" a woman's voice asked. A second later I heard the smacking sound of a fist hitting flesh, followed by a grunt. I clenched my jaw, fighting an urge to barge in. "Who sent you here?" the woman asked, getting louder as Ollie refused to respond.

I looked around the warehouse space, my eye falling on the forklift. It was still parked where the woman had left it, just inside the roll-up door. A plan was formulating in my head, but I needed to be sure I knew where Ollie was situated in the office.

Chains shifted, and I heard a low snarl. "What the hell is that thing?" It was Ollie's voice, the first words I'd heard from him since he was captured. Fear-filled tones, competing with dismay.

"That's my pet," the woman, Darla, said. Her voice dropped into a low purr. I could hear her walking slowly across the room. Chains clanked and then a wet snuffling sound followed her back to where I thought Ollie must be. "Do you like him? He seems to like you."

I'd hoped to have more time, so I could ascertain the location of all the people in the room. But I could tell from Ollie's grunts that the ghoul was getting closer.

I sprinted across the room to the forklift, glad to see the key had been left in the ignition. My experience with the machinery was incredibly limited, but I was familiar enough with them that I knew I could figure this one out. I had to back up to get away from the door, wincing as loud beeps filled the small warehouse.

The office door stayed closed, and I shoved the gear out of reverse as quickly as possible. I pushed the accelerator stick as far as it would go, sending the machine speeding across the warehouse. Keeping it aimed for the part of the office I was certain Ollie wasn't in, I waited until the last moment to jump off and roll across the concrete.

A loud crash filled the air as the forklift plowed through the thin walls of the office. There were several cries of shock and at least one howl of pain. Darla's voice started screeching loudly, a shriek that went on and on.

One of the men stumbled out through the hole in the wall, looking around the warehouse with a glazed expression. I ripped a long plank loose from a pallet, wood that had been attached with a single nail. That nail came out with the plank,

259

though I didn't notice until I was already swinging it through the air. I tried to pull back, but it was too late. The plank hit the man in the back of the head, and the rusty nail buried itself at least an inch into his neck. He dropped bonelessly to the ground.

I held back a shudder as I ripped the nail free, then turned toward the ragged opening. The forklift had turned as it hit the wall, veering toward the location of Ollie's voice. Panic welled up in me, and I feared that I might have hurt him while trying to save him.

Darla came tearing out from the office, her fingers raised in claws. "You killed him!" she screamed, raking her finger-nails across my face. I squeezed my eyes shut protectively, swinging the plank at her ineffectually. She fell back, scream-ing again.

As she launched herself at me one more time, I ducked and caught her stomach with my shoulder. I pumped my legs, shov-ing her backwards until I tripped over some debris on the ground. Her nails scraped along my back as she fell away, and I felt blood welling up under my t-shirt.

My hands were shaking from the adrenaline and nerves as I pushed myself to my feet. Darla's scream had cut off sud-denly, and I saw the cause as I glanced up. I looked with wide eyes at the pool of blood spreading out underneath her. She'd landing on a jagged wooden plank, sticking up from the base-board it had been screwed into. It was long enough that half an inch of the splintery wood was visible, sticking through her side. She'd landed at such an angle that the board had pierced her just above the left hip, passing through her stomach to emerge on the right side of her abdomen. She was groaning and trying to move, held in place by the splintered wood.

Bile rose in the back of my throat, but I shoved down the sick feeling as I stepped over her to enter the office. The last man was laying under a pile of wood and drywall, his head bleeding. He was alive, but I didn't think I'd have to worry about him putting up a fight for several hours at the least.

The ghoul was now my biggest concern. I spotted Ollie, sitting in a chair with his hands zip-tied in his lap. His head was down, but he coughed a few times and then groaned. With a sigh of relief, I hurried over to help him stand. His face was bruised, blood dripping from his nose and a split lip.

"Ollie, are you with me?"

"Yeah, Jack. What the hell just happened?"

"I had to help you, and this was the best I could think of." I waved behind me at the forklift. "Come on, we need to get out of here before that ghoul attacks."

Ollie looked at me with a startled expression. "Jack, I think I saw that thing. I mean, really *saw* it."

A gurgling laugh came from behind me, and I whirled as I dropped into a crouch. The mangled face of the ghoul was only a few strides away, and I tensed in anticipation of his attack. When his snarling face only writhed back and forth, I released my pent-up breath.

The forklift had pinned the ghoul against the wall, one of the tines stabbing through it just under the ribs. The lift was low to the ground, so the ghoul must have been crouching when the machine burst into the office. As I watched in horrified fascination, it twisted back and forth, tearing the gaping wound even more as it tried to get free.

Ollie put a hand on my shoulder. "Is this what you see, Jack? How do you stand it?"

I realized then that we were both seeing the true face of the ghoul. It must have been too injured to maintain the human mask it would normally wear. Its skin was a sickly gray, torn in places and gaping over an eye socket that I now saw was a black void. The ghoul bared its teeth at us, jagged stumps in gums that were an unhealthy shade of red.

"We can't leave it here like this," I said, looking around for a weapon. I finally remembered the plank from the pallet, and I bent to pick it up from where I'd dropped it. "If anyone saw this thing..."

He nodded reluctantly. I knew how much it went against his morals to take justice into his own hands. I raised the board, centered the nail, and then swung it with all of my strength. It took several hits, with the nail striking deep into the ghoul's skull each time, before it stopped writhing and trying to tear itself free from where it was trapped.

Ollie managed to free his hands while I was at work, and he gingerly reversed the forklift several feet. The ghoul was already dead as it flopped to the ground. Its arms and legs were elongated, larger than they should have been. That coupled with the face and strange teeth would scream non-human to anyone who looked closely. I couldn't count on a lazy medical examiner chalking it down as malformed genes or something, as so many Nox had been in the past.

"Help me," I said simply, bending to put my hand under the ghoul's torso. Ollie knelt opposite me to grab its legs, and we lifted it with a grunt. I'd planned to carry it to my car, but after a dozen steps I knew we'd never make it that far.

We dropped the ghoul to raise the warehouse door, and I saw the black SUV parked only a few feet away. I rushed back into the office, patting the pockets of the unconscious Trevor's pants until I found a set of keys.

"They've generously donated transportation," I said, raising them as I returned to the door. The vehicle beeped when I pressed the unlock button, and the rear doors opened automatically after I pressed another button.

Once the ghoul was stuffed behind the rear seats, I passed Ollie my keys. "Call this in. I'm sure the detectives will be ecstatic to find all these stolen drugs, even with all this." I waved to the forklift and the shattered office. "Probably a good idea to make it an anonymous tip."

He chuckled agreement at that. "What are you going to do, Jack?"

"I'll make sure this thing is never found. Better that you don't know any more than that."

He stared at me for several seconds, but finally nodded and turned to walk back to the strip mall where my car was parked, pulling out his phone. He stopped after a few steps, turning to look at me. "I owe you one, Dahlish."

"Call it even," I said with a smile.

It was close to midnight by the time I stepped off a bus outside of Ollie's neighborhood. He had texted me the address, telling me to come by and pick up my car once I was done.

The streets were quiet and empty as I walked past houses filled with sleeping occupants. A few windows had faint light behind them, night owls who I hoped were enjoying themselves much more than I had that evening.

Ollie's house was on a corner lot, with a large front yard that was immaculately maintained. Someone in his family enjoyed gardening, based on the number of bushes and plants that lined the walk and filled the beds in front of the windows to either side of the small porch.

I stood in front of the door, debating whether to ring the bell and risk waking his wife. He'd mentioned kids, too, but I wasn't sure how many or how old they were. I reached out to touch the bell a couple of times, pulling my finger back at the last moment. Each time, I noticed my hand was shaking. I took a steadying breath, leaning back against the cool bricks beside the door.

This was the first time in the two months I'd worn the coin that I'd actually faced a Nox that would have killed me if I hadn't been incredibly lucky. Even while pinned to the wall, that ghoul had been trying to reach me and Ollie with a ravenous hunger on its face.

It was also the second time since I put the talisman on that I'd faced death, the first being a gun pointed at me by the man who'd killed my sister. I was starting to wonder if this was what my life would be like while I was one of the Nine. Could I handle that much excitement?

The door beside me opened and a woman stepped out. She was in her forties, with a lighter shade of dark skin than her husband. Her hair was tied back in a loose bun at the back of her head, and when her amber eyes found me, she smiled warmly. "You must be this Jack Dahlish I've been hearing so much about." She wrapped her arms around me in a welcoming hug, then pulled me into the house. "Ollie told me what you did for him tonight. I can't thank you enough."

Ollie appeared as the door closed behind us, his smile just as wide as his wife's. "I see you've met Sandra."

"I did. It's a pleasure, ma'am." I rubbed the back of my neck in embarrassment at all the attention. "If I can get my keys, I'll get out of your hair. I'm sure you guys are ready for bed."

"Nonsense," Sandra said, her arm around my shoulders still propelling me forward. "You boys worked up an appetite this evening, and I insist that you let us feed you. It's the least we can do."

"How do you like your steak, Jack?" Ollie asked as I entered a cozy kitchen. He was holding a platter with two thick T-bones on it. Just beyond him, I could see through sliding glass doors to a barbecue pit that was smoking in the gentle night breeze. Watching the husband and wife interact, teasing each other as Sandra started to chop up vegetables for a salad, I couldn't help but feel all the tension and worries melt away.

Perhaps friends were an even better thing *after* the fight was done.

About the Author

After more than 20 years of working IT support for a nationwide bank, I decided it was finally time to start putting my imagination to the page. Creating stories and new worlds has been second nature for me since I was a kid, and I've wanted to be a writer since high school.

If you'd like to keep up to date on my projects, visit my website at www.timrangnow.com. You can sign up for my monthly newsletter there and get access to exclusive short stories and early peeks at upcoming books.

Dahlish Series

Lost Souls

Memory and Sorrow

Dark Deception

Fateful Knights

Other Books By Tim Rangnow

Guild Series
Vagabond

Indomitable

Waterloo

Resolute

Rim Jumper
Prime Example

Viridian Skies